AUG 2 4 ~~~~

M000034850

GIBSONS & DISTRICT PUBLIC LIBRARY
BOX 109, GIBSONS, BC   VON 1V0

AUG 2 0 2020

THE ANATOMIST'S TALE:

*Being the confessions of an unwilling pirate,
marooned for a time upon the shores of New Madagascar*

by
Tauno Biltsted

LANTERNFISH PRESS

PHILADELPHIA

THE ANATOMIST'S TALE

Copyright © 2019 by Tauno Biltsted

All rights reserved. No part of this book may be reproduced in any form without permission in writing from the publisher, except for brief quotations used in critical articles or reviews.

LANTERNFISH PRESS

399 Market Street, Suite 360

Philadelphia, PA 19106

lanternfishpress.com

Cover Design: Michael Norcross

Cover Image: "Glitter Path" by Merlyn Chesterman

Printed in the United States of America.

Library of Congress Control Number: 2019943334

ISBN: 978-1-941360-33-0

Digital ISBN: 978-1-941360-34-7

Table of Contents

THE
ANATOMIST'S TALE

ROGUES AND INNOCENTS; OR,
A COMMON TRAGEDY
As told to an investigator of the Admiralty Court

Hail and well met, friend! It is a delight to see your silhouette come dancing along the corridor in the torchlight. Step into the room and hold your torch high so that I can better see the softness of your face. Too long have I been denied the sweetness of the human face; the rough masks worn by the inmates here can scarcely compare. Come in, and let me slyly read you while you crack me open like the pages of a book. Have you been brought here by the rumor that I know the coordinates of jungle cities crusted with jewels, as much as by your duty to determine my complicity in the crimes for which I stand accused? Well, then, I hope I will not disappoint.

Glorious Marshalsea! The cells here—their walls slick with algae and vomit, sweaty with the resigned terror of their occupants—have seen the end of many rogues and more than a few innocents. I would do anything to spare you the unpleasantness of this air, so thick with the stale breath of captivity, but circumstances restrict me to offering only the humble distraction of my wagging tongue. That pile, there? That is a man seized because he bore an unfortunate resemblance to a highwayman who stalked the lanes of Yorkshire; now he lies collapsed and decayed under the king's justice. He is of scant material means and therefore little account, so forlorn that he will scarcely complain if you rest yourself upon him—do not burden yourself with concern for his dignity; he has grown accustomed to his station.

An investigator of the Court must hear it often: "I was a forced man, a victim of circumstance, the product of a vicious childhood; there was no way but for me to pour bitter upon bitter." Or: Firm protestations of innocence, followed by a gallows confession as to the influence of strong drink upon the condemned's sense of judgment and a final bid for the intercession of the attending magistrate, or for a sudden change of heart to overcome the executioner with a burlap potato sack haphazardly obscuring his face.

I hope that you will find more than an echo of other

testimonies in my narrative, and also that you understand my claims to innocence are specific rather than general. In particular: I have never shed the blood of any person outside the bounds of my profession, never engaged in any violence or robbery for my own gain, and never entered into any criminal combination for the purpose of general mayhem or the disruption of trade licensed by the Crown. Finally, I have never once questioned the sovereignty and authority of the Crown—nor of the Admiralty Court, that august body which represents the king in all things maritime, binding the white-capped waters of the distant oceans that lap upon the shores of every continent within the unbreakable chains of English law.

If you hear any shadow of complaint in my discourse, let me assure you that I *prefer* to find myself entombed here in this miasma of shit—transformed from the man I was to the pitiable creature that stands before you, half-starved, intelligence fair drained from my head, straggly of beard and loose of tooth—for it is a better fate than being hanged until dead. Neck stretched by the hangman's noose, soul launched prematurely into eternity; body covered in tar, gibbeted in a cage along the Thames to haunt the water-ways. The hanged man is food for the crows and at the same time a scarecrow to the flock of seamen who flit up and down the Thames, working the white wings of their sails and shouting to the longshoremen at the docks in the course of their interminable journeys. A scarecrow who screams, wordlessly: "Obey!"

I was seized upon a distant sea, material evidence of the reach of English law. Blue waters slapped the edge of the *piragua* as my companion and I scooped water from our sinking vessel. Adrift in the boiling surf, we watched the navy sloop approach with a mix of hope and desperation.

❋

Or rather: I suppose I may as well begin at the beginning, which for all of us alike is between the legs of a woman: covered with generative ooze, dark with the blood of the womb. They tell me I came into the world amid a great, heaving effort and was caught in the able hands of the midwife of the village of Strumpshaw in the west of England, her grip made sure by her attendance at all the births in the region. I was the fourth child of seven born to my mother, Mary Reed Croward—daughter of John Reed, wife of Robert Croward.

As soon as I was old enough, I began to scuttle away from the bustling household and out into the verdant world that beckoned through every chink in the earthen walls. There I made my childish pleasure chasing rabbits through the bushes, collecting salamanders at the edge of the marshy wastes, and following the trails of leaf-brown toads as they made their cautious way through the dusky brush, harrumphing noisily at my unwelcome attention. In those days children of my social class were largely ignored until they became useful to the family: perhaps squeezed, pinched, and tickled lightly in infancy by older siblings hungry as puppies for play; fed scraps, as an afterthought, as they tottered through the house on unstable legs; then put to work as soon as they were able to complete a task reliably (or survive a sound thrashing if they did not). In our earliest years we children were like ghosts, as our survival was by no means assured, but I made my phantom way quite happily, haunting the greening woods and the stubbly fields, getting drunk on rotten fruits and spitting at crows.

We Crowards were a family of tenant farmers, leasing our rocky field and thatch-roofed, mud-brick home from a local landholder. At the start of every month there was a great commotion as every last pocket was turned out and the cobwebbed corners of the house ransacked to pay the rent. When necessary, father Robert labored for the landlord and other large landholders of the area, and the meager household income was also augmented by the sale of butter and cream from our one stringy cow, whom we pastured on the common fields. In good years a pig was sold at Christmastide, having been raised like a prince since he was small and pink.

Once the Croward children reached the age when we could contribute to the family economy, we were charged with gathering all manner of produce from the surrounding landscape, according to the season: watercress from the running streams, wild raspberries, plums and blackberries, crabapples, the mottled eggs of pigeons, walnuts, hazelnuts, and chestnuts that were stored in great burlap sacks to feed the pig through the long nights of winter. We sowed barley and potatoes among the waste lands and returned to harvest them when autumn came. I remember gathering reeds, too, from around the marshes, carrying great bushels of them across the countryside to hang for drying beneath the eaves of our house. We knew they were ready for our mother to fashion into baskets for sale at local markets and fairs when the brown stalks shook with a dry rattle in an easterly wind.

The region of my birth is not known for its natural abundance. The soil, barren by nature, produces a tough and yellowish fodder, bitter on the tongue, and the cattle raised there are good-natured but stunted in their growth, which I guess could also be said of the people if my own slight stature is any indication. While throughout the summer we enjoyed the produce of a little garden as well as a variety of leafy greens and wild herbs such as thyme, balm, and tansy, for most of the year our diet consisted of a porridge made from whatever grain we could produce or acquire and the ubiquitous potato, that wonderful product of the Americas without which I believe the English countryside would be a howling wilderness devoid of human settlement. We supplemented our diet with the skim milk left over from the production of the cream which was sold to pay the rent, along with eggs produced by our few chickens. I recall the bitter albumen and the creamy yoke of a raw egg sucked down in a secret corner where a hen had attempted to hide her nest; we children never once tasted the congeal of a cooked egg, for the eggs, too, were supposed to be sold to service the debts that are the burden of every tenant family. Occasionally, a scrap of cheap bacon found its way into the porridge, but overall there was a dearth of animal food at the table. Thus deprived of the fat and spirituous particles vital for the vigorous health of the human body, the family Croward gauntly faced the daily uncertainties of peasant life.

Robert Croward was not a man prone to fits of melancholy, and Mary was herself the stoic product of a childhood spent in the service of a local dairy farmer. As they were without the luxuries of reflection and literacy, they had no truck with the fashionable approach to child rearing that was spreading through the upper classes when I was young. The philosopher Locke's erudite argument for the importance of education and a softer touch in the breeding of children did not cross the threshold of our home. We were corrected with more blows than words; Robert was not a vengeful man, but he was fierce in his discipline. A nod from him sent the middle children racing out to gather the cow and bring her in to the yard, and we all knew that the passing shadow of a stern mood upon his brow was occasion to hide in the few dark corners of our ragged cottage or out between the hedges. Mary's attention was always focused on the task immediately before her, her watchful gaze alternating between whatever work was at hand and the youngest child clinging to her skirts, so when the weeping and the raging set in it was an uneasy surprise to us all.

It began with an atmosphere audible only to the sensitive ears of children. The youngest became quiet, spooked by an insistent and malevolent crackling like fallen leaves pushed along the lane in an autumn wind. The oldest of the Croward children grew defiant and blustery at the creeping gloom, swelling with youthful indignation against their continued subjugation to the capricious melancholy of their struggling parents, stomping around the house with their bony feet. Stillness reigned over the supper table as we spooned up the weak broth. Our shoulders hunched in anticipation of coming burdens, and the prayer was muttered with a thick and reluctant tongue, followed by a return of the silence that provoked a nauseating tension in the gullet.

The business of government was held of little account in our corner of the realm. Parliament's obscure machinations could not have been further removed from the daily labors of garden and field. The horizon of our lives was close and intimate, confined to the terrain walked in a regular circuit, the quiet of the family in which more was left unsaid than spoken, the pub and the church of the nearest village, and the knowing nods of neighbors who trod the same country lanes. When forced to go into the closest town, Robert traveled in a fog, with a hum in his ears and wisps in his eyes, his senses overwhelmed by the storied buildings breaking the expanse of the sky and the granite cobblestone beneath his feet. He walked with blinders, focused on the quick completion of whatever business was at hand, paying no mind to that clutch of aged milkmaids outside the county magistrate's office, cloaked against the gathering chill of autumn as they protested being denied their customary access to the hills around their village, where they pastured leathery cows who gave sour milk fit only for cheese. Those customary fields had once provided support for the old widows and maids of the village, who scraped together a mean and narrow existence with the sale of milk. Their means of sustenance had been barred to them by the Parliamentary Act for the Enclosure of the Wastes of Norfolk County, which permitted the enclosure of land once subject to the privileges of the commons. A local lord or sheep farmer had only to file duly notarized papers at the magistrate's office and he could fence off whatever he liked.

The mason's apprentice carries bricks on a wooden board fashioned for the purpose, wobbling as weight is added to the load before steadying himself to carry the improbable stack to his master, who sits at the scaffold laying neat beds of mortar and stacking the bricks until the wall reaches its perfect height. If all this had begun slowly, the family Croward might have had the opportunity to compensate in some way, to shift the load so it became bearable; instead, the change arrived all at once in an unexpected torrent.

Ned Croward was my brother. I don't know where he finds himself today, although I have been told that a man of the same name was hanged as a highwayman in Manchester. It is difficult to imagine that could have been him, for he was a slight boy, a little dimwitted, complacent and obedient to a fault—I would sooner have figured him in a poorhouse laboring for his daily bread. He was with Robert Croward that day in the early spring as they walked the muddy lane, a jaunt in their step at the end of winter days that had enveloped us all in the close must of woolen clothing in tight layers against the cold. They set out that morning across the low hills to a spot far from any human habitation, where they intended to prepare a little patch of barley by setting fire to the young spring growth, afterwards digging in the char and spreading seed they carried in a soft rag, lovingly stored up from the past year. As they left the lane to follow the contours of the land they came upon a crude fence with some men leaned up on it who waved Robert off as he approached, saying there wouldn't be any new crops planted this year. A sheep man had applied for those scrubby hills that did not appear on any property register and intended to prepare them for pasture. He had hired these lads to clear the scrub and sow hayseed. They produced a paper in support of their claim, waving it as they spoke, the inky seal black against the green hills behind where the meadow flowers fanned their blues and yellows.

Ned told us how Robert walked up to them saying: "What do you mean, boys? You not being from these parts, why should I pay you any mind?"

Robert was all puffed up like a bantam ready to fight, thin after a lean winter but tough as the life of a tenant farmer makes a man, yet Ned and Robert had nothing with them apart from the implements they would use to start a little fire, while the lads hanging on the fence had thick sticks not meant for planting. They ended up giving Robert a firm whack on his backside after staring him down.

They hang the man and flog the woman
Who steals the Goose from the Common,
But let the greater criminal loose
Who steals the Common from the Goose.

So goes a verse from a song I heard years later, which stuck to me like a burred seed sticks to your clothes as you walk the fields in late summer, when the greenery puts out all manner of contrivance to assure its broadest distribution.

✳

In this cell the passage of the sun is marked by a square of light that moves across the wall up high. The days are punctuated at regular intervals by a chorus of moaning and cursing, filthy jokes, and shouted songs filled with criminal defiance—sea shanties at once bawdy and mournful, full of green-eyed beauties with tendrils of seaweed for hair and tearful weeping for lost loves and frustrated opportunities. Some of them could be my brothers, these men who sing with throats worn raw from shouting over the crash of waves against the hull and the wind whistling through hempen cord and around the canvas sails. I must confess that when I am among them I often search their leathery faces for features I might recognize from my childhood.

The advancement of an anatomical understanding of the body and its operations has served as a model for understanding the wider economy of nature, of which the human body is but one expression. The great anatomist William Harvey, physician to kings, possessed such an inquiring mind that he was not content simply to repeat received truths handed down through the centuries. In his studies on the circulation of blood, Harvey exposed the false premises underlying Galen's theories on the generation of that vital fluid and its passage through the organism. Galen, that god of all anatomists who peers down at us from atop his Roman column, had asserted that blood is generated in the liver, from whence it carries the stuff of life to the organs and tissues in its transit. Galen's faulty premise was that the salty elixir is consumed at its destination, like the rays of the sun falling upon the earth, and that blood must therefore be generated in constant flow by the action of the liver.

William Harvey was curious, and unimpressed by the received wisdom of the ages. By experiment and observation Harvey demonstrated that blood moves through the body on a circulative principle, propelled to complete a swift and regular circuit through every part of the organism. Harvey showed the body to be a balanced and closed system wherein the blood flows bright red through the circuit of the veins, then returns dull and thick along the arteries for replenishment and recirculation through the muscular action of the heart. Every child knows that when a cord is tied tight around a finger, the finger quickly grows numb and takes on a bluish hue. When taken to the extreme, that little experiment can assume morbid proportions, as the limb, removed from circulation and deprived of its necessary replenishment, eventually grows foul—blackened with the brackish blood that, excluded from its circuit, turns poisonous upon the body.

In the late summer of the previous year, Robert Croward had taken the cow to mate with a neighbor's bull, a sedate affair that resulted in a bellowing calf pulled feet first into a dewy spring morning. The neighbor kept his stud bull in hay for the purpose of breeding; year-round that bull stood lowing in the field, his muscled shoulders twitching as he patiently awaited his prizes. Robert hoped to fatten the calf through the summer and sell him come fall, splitting the proceeds with the owner of the bull, a proposition grown urgent after Robert's exclusion from the common fields where he grew the crops that provisioned the family through the long winters, when there was no gleaning to be had.

I was delighted by the gentle, wobbling calf and can still recall the softness of his fur against my face as I reached out my arms to embrace his girth. The little pasture attached to our leased land was quickly depleted by the ruminating cow as her calf stood nestled in her shadow, trying to share of her bodily warmth. When the grass had all been chewed down so that the sandy soil beneath lay bare, I was called on to take the cow and her calf to pasture in the common fields, in hopes that the shifting crowd of hands hired to drive sheep and guard the approaches to the pasture might show more sympathy for a small boy.

I drove the cow and calf along the lane; in their eagerness for a mouthful of fresh grass they were willing charges and followed me like a pair of dogs, but we found every approach blocked. Across each path there was a fence. In the fields a few lads leaned on rough sticks, watching some black-faced sheep of a variety not usually seen in those parts. I could see it was a strain for those lads to maintain the hardness of their hearts. They fixed their gaze in the distance to shield against the sight of my plaintive weeping as I contemplated the thought of returning to my father with our cow still gnawed by hunger, her eyes bugged in desperation as her milk-calf mewled beside her. By midsummer the springtime calf began to sound a low moan at the taste of his mother's watery milk, his ribs a prominent augur to the rapid impoverishment that would descend upon us like a plague.

Trapped within the limited circulation of the little cottage, the Croward family grew desperate. The planting season came and went while Robert made what little he could working at the vast fields of the local landholders. The competition for waged work grew fierce, since all the tenant families in the area found themselves in similar circumstances, required to make the rent while deprived of the means of subsistence that had allowed them some barter with the landholders in previous years, when they might have preferred fetching their own cows out of the pond over mending fences and tending another man's cattle. The marshland was took from us as well, stopping the harvest of the reeds that Mary used to make her baskets and the long heath that she bound tight to a hardened branch of ash to make her besom brooms. Denied the multitude of small enterprises that every family ventured to maintain its meager economy, we were forced to rely wholly on our little garden for sustenance. The potatoes were picked from the ground having barely reached half their mature size, and the cabbage was harvested when it had but a small knot of leaves upon the stalk. Meals became thin concoctions flavored with whatever bitter herbs could be scavenged at the side of the road—in competition with all the other tenant families, who suffered the same grumbling of their bellies. The cow, deprived of fodder, stopped giving milk. Its calf grew weak and sick until the poor thing perished one terrible afternoon in the full blaze of day as the children cast around the yard, restless and exhausted.

Robert Croward grew agitated and prone to lash out, reminding me of the bears that accompanied the traveling people who, in better seasons, set up their ragged tent in an open field, sending word of invitation far and wide for all the peasant families to come and watch their show for a little bit of coin. The travelers fanned out through the area to sell pots and pans, hauling along a portable grinding stone that they used to sharpen knives and farming implements in exchange for a pot of milk or a bag of potato flour. On certain evenings they set their bears to dance under chain to the delight of all the children. The bears were amiable enough as they stood on their hind legs and danced, although occasionally they sent the children squealing and scuttling when they tired of their play, roaring and slapping at their keepers until quieted by the crack of the whip.

Robert Croward was a quiet man; though he ruled his days with steady and unwavering effort, he was unconditioned to the expression of his feelings. In that harsh season, his face grown thin and lined, he yelled at his wife at dinner one night with disgust.

"Why do you put water at the table and call it soup?"

We all lapped at the thin broth, intent on drawing from it whatever nourishment could be had.

"Is it too much to ask for a piece of bread, or to taste a little fat floating at the top?"

Mary's own helpless rage made her respond with a string of curses and insults, sharp and precise cuts that served to whittle away the regard in which I had held my parents. A blur of quick blows sent Mary to her knees, still cursing in fury. The chairs were upended and our few earthenware bowls shattered upon the floor, until at last Robert stalked out the door to drive the family a little further into debt with a mug or two of the hop-rich beer that filled the village pub with its sour, floral air. Later that season our father took himself to East Anglia in search of employment, and that was the last we saw of him: walking with a determined stride, far up the lane and away from the home where I was born.

It was a bitter harvest season. We all began to wither as we went about our days. The children's hair grew coarse and ragged as we walked the lanes, gathering what edible plants we could and stripping the cob nuts off of the hedge rows, our bellies distended from sucking air and drinking huge quantities of water from the stream to quell our hunger. Come harvest time, the cow was sold for a paltry sum; she was dragged out of the yard with her bony hips plain for all to see, pulled behind the man who bought her, her spirit resolved to the slaughterhouse, seemingly deaf to my tearful complaints.

Mary attempted to supplement the loss of wages, crops, and milk by taking on what cottage work she could, but she had never been a seamstress and tended to bloody the garments while going half-blind, sewing at the rough kitchen table by the sun's natural light and well into the night by the flickering flame of a single candle. Her eyes became inflamed with pain by the force of her concentration. At times she seemed to fold into herself, beginning at the squint in the middle of her brow. At the end of the harvest we had a burst of full pots as we gleaned what we could from the picked-over fields—a traditional arrangement maintained in poor recompense for the loss of our rights to common fields and pasture.

There are a number of men in Parliament, supported by economists and commentators of high regard, who advocate the ongoing enclosure of the common lands, where the grasses grow long and languorous between the scattered plantings of the landless tenant farmer; where the whistling of the wind through the long reeds of the fen is accompanied by the splash of fish, the croaking of frogs, and the sawing of crickets rubbing their chitinous limbs; and where families of little means drive their stock animals to grow fat. Those experts in public affairs see fit to declare these provinces of shared account to be virtual wastelands of little profit, whose trifling fruits fall from the tree spent and withered. They would prefer to impose a rational and scientific order on that wild territory, much like what prevails in the Midlands as they are found today, where sheep graze fields that blanket the ruins of empty villages and stands of wispy-topped corn sway in uniform depth like a great lake spread across the hills. The experts even claim it is the poor who will finally benefit most from this reordering of the countryside—a claim which flies directly in the teeth of the landless classes' own feelings, for who would not prefer to eat the cheese of his own cow over slaving in the city to earn a few pence with which to buy some oily crust?

✳

My eighth birthday, falling in the early weeks of the new year, came and went with little notice. Mary had grown sick with grief at the death of her youngest child, a sad-faced girl who had barely learned to walk, and who turned pallid as we all huddled beneath our woolens in the long, dark days of winter. Denied the right of turbary, we had no peat, so were forced to rely on the ghostly blue flames put out by the few faggots of sticks we had gathered, supplemented by sheep dung spirited out of the fields. It was days before we took my little sister's body to the pastor, her slight form already stiff with death, the cheeks turned blue.

Spring arrived with a flourish that was quickly stripped by the rush of hunger that burst out of all of the houses of the region, as the new shoots were harvested by scores of filthy little hands scouring the roadsides and sneaking into fields in search of any tender leaf that looked palatable. There were numerous cases of poisoning as any manner of life uncovered by the receding mantle of frost went into the soup pot with little heed to traditional lore concerning the produce of field and forest. Bird song was stilled by flocks of boys and stick-thin women armed with rocks, their aim grown true with desperate bursts of mental calculation and surety of purpose. Little creatures with barely a smidgen of flesh on them were roasted whole, their bitter meats taken along with the crunch of bone.

Stray dogs plagued the countryside that spring, as households that had kept an animal for the delight of the children or for practical service could no longer afford to feed an extra mouth. Those mascots were put out to fend for themselves, crying as they clawed at doors and sulked around sheds, begging to be let into the only homes they had known. Chased away again and again in a hail of stones, the dogs grew feral and made their way into the marshlands, where they ate frogs, chased what quick rabbits had managed to avoid the soup pot, and caught fish and burrowing worms as best they could. The dogs mated with the ferocity of the dispossessed to produce litter upon litter of pups that quickly grew big and hungry to haunt the country lanes with yellow eyes and bared fangs; the youngest children were advised not to walk about without a cudgel and a pocket full of stones.

Stunned by the enormity of the devastation, Mary Croward took her family to the town of Norfolk, where for a time we lived on the outskirts in a misery so abject it is difficult for me to recall. The days seemed to unfold in a persistent haze of weariness and disbelief. The family Croward, always of less than noble origin, was soon no more after Mary failed to return from one of the nightly rounds that brought her home drunken and abused but with a little coin tucked away on her person. What little solidarity remained among the Croward children had ebbed as we filched what we could from one another and competed for the affections of addled Mary and the extra crumbs it might bring. Within a week of her departure, familial bonds had grown so light and ephemeral that they dwindled to the point of disappearance. The oldest among us crossed the threshold with nary a backward glance, making a little traveling sack with whatever we could grab. Throughout the day the rest slowly filtered out of the hovel we had never called home.

God's Graceful Creatures;
or, a Butcher's Tale
As told to a representative of the Surgeons' College

To be orphaned at the age of nine is to stand alone amidst a multitude, boyish cheeks still fat with youth and stained from dodging the tramping feet and idle blows of adults who, being outside of any bonds of familiarity, view the orphan as simply competition, to be extinguished with less thought than one would give to blowing out a candle at the end of the evening. A young boy alone in the world can employ himself in any number of occupations—for instance, as a shoeblack who carts a rough box in the crook of his arm as he wanders the streets with rags and polish, begging the privilege of shining the shoes of gentlemen, learning from his mates the trick of making the rag squeak just so against the boot to bring out the spit-shine—all to earn a rough sleep slumped on the stone steps, a wearing pain in the side, and hands stained with boot polish, even the palms blackened to show he is an outcast. When properly bred into the occupation, a nimble-fingered shoeblack can acquire the particular talent of emptying the contents of a waistcoat pocket while the customer looks at his watch—a skilled boy knows how to leave no trace of his filthy fingers anywhere except on the bottle of gin that he clutches with both hands as night falls.

The climbing boy is engaged in a similarly filthy profession—exchanging the shine of bootblack for the deep charcoal of a chimney flue—and it turns him sooty and sulfurous like some creature of the netherworld until he, too, is an outcast except among his own small brotherhood of boys like himself. Or a boy can simply beg—become one more bit of flotsam in the choked tides that wash upon the streets of every town in the nation of England in daily transit. Of girls—cursed by that gentle gash between their legs, a subtle sign of the wonders of the reproductive system that it mouths, provoking a curious and brutal hunger in the minds of men—of girls I can only speculate. Girls thrown upon the mercy of the street bob like froth upon the ocean until they vanish or are replaced by painted likenesses of themselves, grown hard and foul-mouthed against their daily assault.

✻

It was a few short days before I grew disoriented and hungry, haunting the streets and alleyways of Norfolk, fighting with rats and other children for scraps of food, seeing phantoms of my poor mum at every turn, and hoping desperately that the blank entreaty of my hungry eyes might persuade a bit of overripe fruit to fall into my hands from the tables of the market ladies who sat and gossiped behind their mountains of produce. It was six weeks' time until the morning when a young gentleman of noble disposition approached me in the street, asking if I had slept in a bed that night. I looked up at him and shook my head. Even now I can recall seeing a halo around his face. He grabbed my arm and marched me through the streets until we arrived at the threshold of the parish poorhouse, where he banged with his walking stick. A man came to the door still in his nightclothes; he had a pained expression until he saw who it was. The gentleman handed me over to this director without a word, although I saw that they exchanged a wink and a bit of coin.

I was indentured within a short time of my arrival at the poorhouse—sold for eight years of service at the age of nine and a half, head still spinning with the recent loss of my familial bonds. I winced at the grip of the butcher's wife as she led me away.

"Now, now, boy, there's no reason to worry. The work's

Gibsons & District Public Library
604-886-2130

not too hard, the trade is good, and there is always food to be had."

I looked at her hand as she spoke and saw that her gloves were frayed at the edges. "Yes, ma'am."

Her words came to me as if I were at the bottom of the ocean, the needle of my internal compass flitting among the near-forgotten names of my mother, father, and siblings: a jumble of muttered consonants.

"We are good people and kind, and you will be like a son to us. The child we never had." Her other hand, the one not holding mine, brushed absentmindedly at her belly. "Though of course we have also taken you on to work, and work you shall." She tightened her grip.

"Yes, ma'am." I gazed up at her round face, which hung over me like a moon at midday, and nodded assent, though I scarcely understood what was being discussed.

❋

While it is true that the trajectory of my career has been most unusual, it is not entirely without precedent. Even Galen himself—that first among physicians, who made his name bleeding the august senators of Rome—peered past the veil of the skin to dissect the organs of pigs, goats, and horses, finding the structures that repeat themselves with variation, the packages of muscle that animate the skeletal structure, the network of veins and arteries that carry blood throughout the body, the reproductive organs that assure the replication of the species, the yards of intestines to filter the wheat from the chaff in alimentation. The round-faced ape was his subject for investigations of the brain and nervous system. He had the animals throttled with a wire to ensure the veins were not overly constricted as they died. Galen's investigations revealed the gossamer filaments that connect us to the world: the large nerves of the eyes, the ears, and the tongue; the whole system of nerves that infiltrates its threadlike structures throughout the flesh in a fine web, transmitting the impulse of the animal spirits along its tendrils, without which we would be dumb creatures, lumps of flesh insensible to the glories and desolations of the surrounding world.

There is almost no place that I prefer to the theatre of dissection, finding its exercise of the mind to be a practice of spiritual dimensions. Which is no small irony, given that I might soon land upon the dissection slab myself, if I am indeed sentenced to have my neck cracked before a middling crowd at Executioner's Dock, condemned as a pirate even as I protest my innocence to the heckling mob who calmly chew on sweets and boiled potatoes. I can clearly conjure the moment, standing with you over my own corpse upon the table, the face removed as a courtesy by the attending anatomist: a small, though appreciated, gesture in honor of my prior attendance at the College. Our tongues click quietly in our mouths and we tuck our hands behind our backs as we roll lightly on the balls of our feet—keeping our bodies supple to ensure that our powers of observation are at their height.

I have washed the bodies of convicted men bloated from the tides of the Thames, where they were dunked three times in ritual observance of the sovereignty of the Admiralty Court. I have prepared them for dissection in the theatre, giving them a purpose they never envisioned: to serve the incremental advancement of science. Yes, I have washed the Thames's too-sweet water—an insult to their history—from the salt-battered bodies marked with rough tattoos, mangled fingers, faces lined beyond their years. I have heard their spirits whisper, calling for the sunken currents of the ocean, demanding that the hammock which swung them in life be sewn once again around their bodies, obscuring their features as they are consigned to the deep where the cold water will insinuate itself into the fibers of the caul, prying their eyes open with its insistent pressure as they are salted away in fields of anemone and starfish.

There remain distinctions between the country butcher's shop and that of the city butcher who cuts and apportions meat for all of London. In London, all provisions of animal flesh are procured through Smithfield, where the visitor who approaches from the lane will find ponds of steaming blood, heaps of rotting offal, and streams of waste full of hair and bits of flesh from the scalding of the freshly killed animals. The country butcher shop is a smaller affair, where there is no truck with bummarees who grow strong carrying bony carcasses upon their backs. In a country butcher shop the smaller scale of the enterprise allows the butcher to select the livestock for slaughter, examining the animals at market, checking them for illness, and observing the firmness of muscle and clarity of eyes as they bleat and low in full expression of their animal qualities, still ignorant of their destiny to end at the dining table—to be cut at the joints, muscle carefully removed from bone, organs cleaned and processed for sausage, stomachs turned inside out, intestines stretched and washed for casings. Even the drained blood, black and rich, will be saved for pudding.

My master was a thick man with generous, ruddy cheeks and soft brown eyes that grew colder and smaller as he aged. He had come into the trade of butchery through the graces of his father, who had done well for himself putting fine cuts on the tables of the lords, wholesalers, barristers, and master tradesmen of the region and also made a fair bit of coin selling bacon to the working families, who would buy small portions to flavor their porridge when they could afford it. He was not a cruel master—warm in his own way, gregarious with his clients and anticipating their needs, placing aside certain cuts favored at the one household, smoking the calf livers just so for the other. He was convivial with the servants who came to purchase for their wealthy mistresses and the washerwomen who came looking for a bit of scrap. Outside of the shop he was quieter, typical of men of a certain age who seem limited to a greyish spectrum of emotions, animated only by a tepid heat. His failure to beget a family did not leave the butcher too embittered to place a warm hand upon my shoulder as he directed me to get the haunch for smoking or work the gears for the grinder. His relationship with his wife was still cordial when I entered the household as a young indenture, although in time the continued failure of their couplings to produce heirs to his empire of meats dampened the dim flame of affection between them.

"The meat is better if you calm the animal before slaughter," the butcher said. He demonstrated by placing a firm and steady hand behind the pig's ear, holding the enormous grunting animal with a sure touch before procuring from an apron pocket a long knife, which glinted in the low light of the shed like a comet in its transit before swiftly slicing through the pig's neck. A stream of blood pulsed onto the pounded earth floor, which was already blackened with the lifeblood of countless beasts. The blood puddled luminescent before growing a dull coagulant skin, the reflection of the room caught in its dark surface, as I and the other boys hoisted the dying animal up by its hind legs, the body warm and shuddering but offering no resistance as its animate qualities subsided, the splatter falling like molten metal—thick, liquid, and warm.

An animal killed when in a state of high anxiety will have a noxious quality to its meat: the cow bellowing in fear, eyes bulging from the skull as the tongue hangs swollen and frothy from between its lips; the pig darting and leaping while letting out a panicked squeal; ululating goats crying like babies as they scramble for a solid footing. The meat derived from a pig slaughtered in the wrong conditions is soft and crumbly to the touch, a disgrace upon any butcher's counter—not even fit for sausage, as it results in a watery sack that cannot be spiced or blended.

It may have been the result of her inability to bear children, or it may have been some other infirmity that rocked the seat of her sensible parts, but the butcher's wife suffered her days in a manner I had not witnessed before. The butcher and his wife lived above the shop, in a small flat with no separate wing for servants. The washing and the cooking was performed by girls who came and went, which left me frequently alone in the close quarters of the house with the butcher's wife, for the butcher himself was often absent. As a prominent man in the town, he had a regular calendar of engagements and many obligations to the society of men.

In the solitude of the home the moods of the butcher's wife found their flower, spreading viny tendrils through all the rooms, and I daily returned from my appointed work uncertain of what I might encounter. On some days a dull, grey atmosphere blanketed the whole place, heavy as dense wool. I would find the curtains drawn close against the antiseptic light of the sun and the butcher's wife disheveled, still in her bedclothes, crouched on the floor and moaning a litany of distress. In this state she exhibited an inordinate fear of being touched, recoiling with a sickened shiver if I drew near to offer the simplest consolation. She thought herself fragile, convinced that the limbs at her side were made of glass and subject to shattering, and she refused any attempt to guide her towards her bed. Instead, she languished against the wall in an inconsolable terror, her face transformed from an aspect healthful and serene to a pale mask of itself. The butcher was incapable of meeting her in these moods. He averted his gaze upon seeing her face lined with the strain of unseen horrors, often returning his hat to his head to walk the night a bit, hoping that before his return she would slip back into her room or otherwise out of his sight.

Other times, the pendulum of her affliction would swing towards the opposite pole, from the deepest melancholia to an excess of energetic agitation, and at these times it was as if there was a wind that blew through the house, flapping at the curtains and lifting the door mat, no subtle breeze but a whirlwind. In the days of high energy the servant girls would throw down their work, alarmed by their mistress' ravings, tossing their aprons upon the floor in a hurry as they rushed out the door. When she was thus undone, the butcher's wife could not channel the surges that coursed through the passages provided by nature and the banks of her river overflowed, inflaming her nerves with a sensuality that left her quivering and hot to the touch with the quickening blood underneath. In the early years of their marriage, when his wife was in such a state, the butcher would relent, and their couplings would shake the house with the ferocity and destructive force of a flood. Later, however, he grew weary of this phase of her affliction as well.

I recall all manner of games that began with a cloying voice calling to me. As a young man bereft of guidance or example, I was unable to discern the improper nature of her attachment to me, yet that voice prompted a sickening turn in my gut like an overly sweet tea, with the same indulgent smack of pleasure and a tightening in that muscle below the gut that tickled and ached at the same time. It was always a tumble, furtive and dark. She would lead me under her skirts with an imploring whine, and I would comply—confused, at first, as any boy would be, but I learned to find the secret fruit concealed within the spread of her white legs, pushing my mouth against it as the flesh of her thighs molded itself around my body and she thrust into me with quick movements, heaving and sighing all the while.

❄

I have heard there is a clock in the city of Strasbourg that reproduces perfectly the motion of the cosmos using a system of gears and wheels: the sun stable and unwavering at the center, the planets completing regular circuits around it upon their worn and eternal paths. The device winnows all that happens throughout the vast coldness and disorientation of space down to a simple mechanical rotation around a tangible point.

I have also had occasion to observe the movements of the celestial bodies through a telescope, seeing with my own eyes how they are suspended by the occult forces of gravitation theorized by Sir Isaac Newton. I felt myself float in the blackness of space as I watched Mars moving through a field of stars on a clear evening. It may have been that I was unaccustomed to the instrument or that my eyes were untrained to the action of the lens, but I noticed a flicker in the steady light of the stars and a certain wobble in the movement of the planet.

✳

I found that I had a natural curiosity as to the inner workings of the creatures that came to me in the butcher shop, the discrete pieces of them hinting at functions beyond being turned to nightsoil in the gullets of men. I began to study my meats as a mechanic might examine the disassembled parts of a machine. I was enthralled by the slick, grey organs with their variety of purposes, their different tissues and placements in the body: the lungs hiding the delicate fruit of the alveoli, the long and knotted intestines coiled like a nest of snakes palpitating in the central cavity, the muscular heart that rested tense in my hand when a pig was freshly killed, slippery with the fading spirits of animation. I was fascinated with the puzzle of bones forming a lattice for the flesh, without which we would all be worms oozing along the ground, and with the ankle, whose intricate strength lets the ox suspend its great bulk to pull the plow in the field, and with the articulate hip, which gives the pig such surprising agility.

My curiosity enhanced my skill, and I became my master's foremost apprentice, the only one allowed to prepare the finest cuts of meat for his richest customers. The butcher did not protest when I asked to be allowed to work the slaughterhouse as well, to learn how to make the primal cuts. There, I deepened my understanding of the animal body as I watched life fade from the freshly killed beasts. Careful to preserve the commercial viability of each carcass, I took what opportunity I could to peel back the skin and reveal the bundles of muscle that animated the creature, the intricate bone work in the ear, the parts of the reproductive system, and their relation to each other. I observed the ducts that lead to the cow's teats, providing milk; the muscles around the brow and cheek that blink the lids of the pig's eyes; the soft cartilage between the bones of the spinal column; the bundles of nerves at the base of the neck. I began to document my haphazard observations with little illustrations and written accounts, rife with the poor grammar and crabbed hand that I had learned to aid in keeping accounts in the butcher shop. The butcher indulged me, amused perhaps by the eccentric indenture acquired for a pittance at the poorhouse, whose predilections were coming to their full and morbid flower with the onset of a certain maturity.

What possessed the butcher to display my illustrations, painstakingly rendered with the static precision of the self-taught, I cannot say, but one day they appeared pinned on the wall of the shop when I entered in the morning. It was apparent that he had spent some time rifling through the blood-splattered pile of sketches, since the works displayed were the ones I had myself taken the most pride in.

"Hullo, boy," my master said, his customary morning greeting accompanied by a blast of hot breath, his whiskers arching with a smile. I scuttled to the back room to load the stock up at the counter; his touch fell lightly on the back of my head as I passed him where he stood. I later gazed at those figures upon the wall, mesmerized, as I pushed sawdust across the floor with a broom. Illustrations traced in India ink on white sheaves, pinned there like moths captured in their nighttime fluttering: they seemed to me as if made by another hand, not my own.

In the past it was only royalty who kept a cabinet of curiosities to demonstrate their wealth and nobility by collecting examples of the dazzling abundance of the natural world: gems and minerals of rare and unusual hue, stuffed birds of exotic plumage, the skeletons of rare beasts whose fleshed-out form has never been observed, animal skins, the desiccated feet of elephants, clockwork automata and other mechanical creatures, the spiral horn of the narwhal once thought to be that of the fabled unicorn. The current popularity of the scientific method has made such collections more common, and the market for such goods and related ephemera has become more extensive. Some of the customers at the butcher shop began to inquire about my little drawings—they were unusual enough to catch the eye—and eventually a collector of oddities passed through and asked if he might buy some, thinking there might be a market for them in London. Being no fool, the butcher began to encourage my predilections by granting me ample time to document my dissections. My anatomical illustrations improved, and in time my drawings became known to more serious collectors.

My indenture was near its end when I was told of an opportunity to study at the Surgeons' College. My self-directed studies had gained me some renown, and the College had certain arrangements for students with talent but no means. I gratefully accepted my position as subsizar, which left me free to pursue my studies whenever I was not emptying bedpans or performing minor services for proper, paying students and gentlemen.

There are many applications of the surgeon's art to daily life's onslaught upon the body: the cautery of wounds, the removal of gangrenous limbs grown black and heavy with infection, the setting of bones snapped in the course of the body's progress through space, the removal of bladder stones, the binding of hernias, the pulling of teeth amidst much writhing in the chair. Every surgeon will tell you, though, that it is on the field of battle where his art faces its greatest challenge: staunching the flow of blood from a body run through with a blade or bullet, bandaging a crushed jawbone or mangled hand. It is war that trains the instincts of the surgeon to make quick decisions. Attempt to save a limb, or remove it? Which of the wounded might survive, and which will surely die from their injuries? And all of this occurs in the midst of pitched battle, the roar and the flash. For a surgeon seeking to make his name, it is war that presents an opportunity of immeasurable advantage for learning the intricacies of the human body and the outrages that can be committed upon it.

Upon finishing my studies at the Surgeons' College, I was adept at mimicking the accent and manner of the educated classes. However, I had no means to set myself up in practice, and no connections. In the absence of a conflict between nations, I determined to complete my training in the practical application of the surgical arts upon the decks of a merchant vessel, where the labor of men places them at war with the elements, and the possibility of sudden and catastrophic injury presents itself with an assuring regularity.

Rhinoceroses; or, the
Shambles of Language
As told to a maid in the employ of our narrator's sister

It was the bright and clear morning of June 20, 1721, when I signed a contract to work as shipboard surgeon on the Royal Fortune. A colleague from the Surgeons' College whose father was an investor in various merchant ventures had informed me of the position. My colleague knew that I lacked family connections, and it was a kindness when he told me about the opening. Upon hearing the news I rushed back to my room to pen a list of my qualifications, which were scant at the time, but my note of inquiry was nonetheless accepted. The letter of invitation that I received was written in a rigid, blockish script on thin and waxy paper similar to what a butcher uses to wrap his chops. I was directed to the worn offices of an aged solicitor whose whiskers were yellow with tobacco and spit.

My colleague had informed me that the sloop would traverse the Atlantic on a route that had seen the regular passage of a half-century's trade. It would carry brass manufactures, textiles—including several large bales of silk—and earthenware to the West Indies for sale and trade in the markets there. At the Caribbean ports the ship would take on bricks of sugar and great barrels of molasses to be transported along the American coast to the colonies of New England, and for the return voyage to London the hold would be packed with rum, furs, cotton, and great bales of hemp. The journey was expected to end with sailing up the Thames at a low tide some thirteen months after our initial departure, good weather and steady currents permitting.

When I pushed through the door of the solicitor's office, a strange man with a back rigid as a tombstone stiffly thrust his hand at me. I thought him a captain or an officer by the deep lines etched into his face from years of squinting at the sun and the awkward, martial bearing that spoke of command. As I greeted him he nodded, his eyes burning under the bird's nest of his brow as he said, "Let me introduce myself—I am Bellamy, the captain of the ship. I like to take the measure of every man who is to serve under me." His eyebrows quivered, his palm leathery and hard against my own as he squeezed with affected vigor.

My compensation would be a small share of the voyage's profit, the routine method of payment for officers and surgeons on a merchant venture. Common sailors contract their wage in coin, a fixed rate of compensation for the duration of the voyage, usually a pittance with subtractions for any costs incurred that leaves just enough for the sailor to wash up on the docks of London still dripping with the salt spray, treat himself to a few days in the bawdy house and some sour pints, and then land once more on the rough boards of the dock like a cat come for a bowl of milk, begging to be signed on for the next long haul. Sailors speak in bitter terms of the times when they are robbed of even the meager wage for which they contract. If a common tar jumps ship in a foreign port—no matter that he flees starvation or abuse at the hands of the ship's commander—he loses any claim to payment, with no reference to the extent of his labors prior to his departure. A sailor risks this penalty if he departs at any time during the voyage, and even after he has sailed a full round and unloaded the last of the cargo from the hold, as the corporation funding the merchant venture may collude with the captain to cite an obscure statute or claim violation of the terms of the contract in order to deny the sailor his fair due, thereby increasing their own respective shares of the profit. The sailor, having little recourse to justice, is left to beg his way onto another ship, where at least he might be fed.

"We are pleased to have you aboard, Surgeon, and expect you will fulfill your duties with the utmost precision," said Captain Bellamy. I was too elated at having assured my position with the flourish of my signature to think much of the strained grimace that contorted his features.

✳

The Royal Fortune was a two-masted merchant sloop, her fading rails once painted a lustrous red. The black-tarred hull rode proud and high on the water when I first saw it, before it was weighted down by the cargo that the grunting dockmen stacked with precision in the hold. Her ragged sails were weather-beaten but seaworthy, for the tar who mended them was a Hindu who could have been a seamstress judging by the tightness of his stitch. Built as a merchant ship, the Royal Fortune had largely plied her trade in the waters of the North Atlantic, with an occasional side run of barrels of dried cod to the ports of the Baltic Sea, to the slender spires of Riga, and the shimmer of Stockholm. The longest haul prior to my fateful voyage was a load of good English earthenware carried to Marseilles against the wishes of the crew, who grumbled about the threat of corsairs as leverage to insist on higher pay. The ship had four cast-iron guns, their tarnished barrels lurking impotently at portholes cut roughly into the side of the hull.

When I came upon the Royal Fortune as she was being loaded, the work chantey rang out along the worm-eaten pier as cargo swung through the air. All the river pilots in their skiffs clustered next to the ship, hoping one of those pallets would crash into the shallow waters so they could flock upon it like screeching gulls, seizing what they could before the patrols came to chase them off.

At any given time there are thousands of ships clustered along the Thames—bobbing in the tides as they push into their docks like pups at a bitch's teats. At Wapping the water slaps the sides of the ships. Sails creak and sway; cargo piles up on the docks in a profusion of towers, teetering great crates fashioned and refashioned for the transport of goods from all parts of the world. The scrawl of a thousand tongues marks the rough surfaces of crates holding enormous bales of English calico wrapped in burlap; great hogsheads of tobacco from the Americas; aromatic tea from Ceylon; and small barrels of bright curry spices grown in the hills of Tamil Nadu and pounded to dust in the back alleys of Mumbai. You will even see clutches of African slaves, some still wearing the tattered garments and braided hair of the homes they were taken from. It is all of a piece in the great chain of commerce that links ports and entrepôts across the expanse of the globe.

The voyage of even the most everyday commodity requires a vast system of cooperation: somewhere the field worker coaxes the green shoot from the ground; the mule driver takes it to port; the dockworkers gather in the hall waiting to load the next shipment; the seaman adjusts the rigging to catch the breath of wind that might propel his ship across the oceans; the stars in the sky make their constant and measurable transit that allows for the triangulation of position, if not purpose, through the watery expanse. The lady of the house at the dry goods store surveys the shelves with their neatly stacked packages, checking their contents against her list, without contemplating the origin of the powdered coffee, the fine sea salt, the tobacco for her gentleman, the soap powder. She merely unclasps the button of her purse—its ivory gotten from the tooth of an elephant hunted in her old age, the spear a pointed insult against a long life—a tooth cut on the African savannah and traded to a caravan en route to the ports of West Africa, where it was bundled and sold in exchange for English textiles, thus joining the long and wave-swept round of purchasing cheap to sell dear.

The morning of my departure, I said goodbye to the lady who ran the boarding house where I had lived since beginning my studies. I sent a note to the butcher and his wife, telling them I would call on them upon my return from far-flung shores. My few belongings were packed into one small trunk: surgical equipment, some key medical texts, a monograph on the flora of the British possessions in the West Indies (which I had purchased after much deliberation, as the cost was prohibitive to my limited income), and a few empty notebooks in which I thought to record my impressions. I had provided the captain with a small list of supplies to procure on my behalf, and I carried with me one extra suit and one broad-brimmed hat that I thought might help in the equatorial climes where I had heard the sun burned with such ripe intensity. I wish now that I could feel again the scratch of that suit against my skin—it was never in fashion and a terrible costume for a sea voyage, its finespun wool quickly reduced to threads by the salt spray and constant wear, but those threads would be silk next to the greasy rags that cover me now.

When I announced Wapping dock as my destination, the carriage driver inquired as to the details of my voyage. He said that he himself was a former seaman.

"It is a good thing you are employed as a surgeon, for the lot of a seaman is a hard one, nothing but work and the oblivion of drink to soothe the strained muscle." The bulge of his forearms and his smashed face signaled a life of hard work, but even as he bemoaned the seaman's life I sensed in his words a certain longing.

"Is there anything of it that you miss? Or do you entirely prefer the life of a carriage driver?" I asked, to see if I might draw him out and learn a bit more about the journey that lay ahead of me.

"There is a wildness to the wide ocean, an awe that comes with sailing up to foreign shores, and there is something sweet about the company of hard men bred to seafaring," he said with a sigh, "but I became a family man. The lot of a carriage-driver has its sorrows too, but I prefer to see the seasons turn upon my brats rather than think on them from afar."

Wapping town struck me as a sorry collection of taverns and timber yards, dancehalls and bawdy houses. The buildings there seemed provisional and impermanent, the tenements and cottages of a most inferior construction—scarcely a brick house among them. There is an air of transience to the place; all the residents of Wapping are dedicated to the trade and service of the docks. There are the sailors and their home port wives, grocers, tavern keepers, no end of strumpets and trulls displaying their wares on the Ratcliffe Highway, filthy children clambering in streets choked with debris and excrement, and great, healthy pigs rooting in the piles of refuse. A foul breath rises from the marshes that ring Wapping, permeating the air.

I peered out the window of the carriage, imagining salt breezes against my face and the chop of the ship breaking the waves. At the dock the carriage driver helped me with my trunk, then stood about taking in the foul air with flared nostrils before ambling off along the dock, clicking his tongue at his horse. It was with great anticipation that I enquired with the dockmaster as to the slip where the Royal Fortune waited to begin her mission: to be pushed by the wind and the scurry of men in slow and laborious transit across the breadth of the Atlantic.

I stood at the top of the gangplank listening to the roll of the ship and the song of the sailors as they loaded the hold and prepared the vessel for departure. I waited for the captain expectantly, hoping for a handshake and a slap on the back to welcome me aboard. I stood there for quite a while, my kit at my side, until a sailor passed with a length of rope in his arms.

"You the surgeon?"

I said yes, hoping that he had been sent to bring me to the captain.

But he only pointed down a darkened stair and said, "Yours is the second on the left; make yourself comfortable as you can."

"And the captain?"

"He's finishing some business ashore." The sailor walked away briskly, wholly uninterested in easing my discomfort.

✻

I hope that you are able to convey to my sister the underlying substance of my tale and not simply a report of my strange aspect, ruined by the interminable purgatory I suffer here in Marshalsea, where I must conjure ghosts to pass the time while I lay rotting upon a pallet of straw like some mad Ottoman. By the sway of your back and the muscle of your arm I imagine you a girl accustomed to hard service, who, like any good servant, must be keen to the subtleties of expression of those you serve. By the clockwork turn behind your eyes I can see that despite the tight draw of your lips and your crystalline silence you listen and record my ramblings—I only ask for you to take note of not only the broad arcs that I trace but also the currents that run beneath the gross thickness of my wandering tongue. I hope that you will not take offense, but I must tell you that your face is pretty, in a sallow way. Would you offer me a small gift? Draw closer, so I can capture your scent and the silhouette of your figure hidden beneath your shawl. Those fond memories would sustain me for days.

If you will not grant me those little favors, I would only ask, even beg on my knees if they were not ruined for kneeling, that when you depart with my good wishes you do not forget to whisper to the guards that I have word of a place that I encountered in my journeys, a place where the natives paint themselves with gold in sparkling homage to the sun, whom they think a god in daily rotation about his dominions. It is a place where the lake bottoms are caked with gold dust and the hills brilliant and sparkling with all manner of gems, the shards near blinding in the bright light of the morning. If you would mention this I would greatly appreciate it, as I hope to arrange a meeting with the governor to bargain for my freedom. I have been here more than half a year now, and in that time have seen a number of men condemned to hang, launched into eternity after their walk through the prison yard—some defiant, colorful with ribbons and drunk against the judgment rendered on them—others in somber parade, faces pegged to their feet until they close their eyes at the noose. If I could I would avoid that final drop, or at least delay it until I grow old and grey.

✳

The Royal Fortune eased out from the cluster of ships, taking two days to meander down the estuary of the Thames, past the town of Gravesend, and into the Channel. When I saw the mouth of the Thames opening up into the wide waters I panicked at the thought that I was passing beyond the bounds of what little world I had known, in a company of men not one of whom knew my name. I felt as if a fog was risen up between me and the other men on the ship; as I strained to make sense of what was around me, I found understanding as elusive as mercury. I had not been raised for seafaring; my family is of peasant stock, rooted in smallholding on the rocky soil and the husbandry of bony cows and half-feral pigs. I had no lore of life at the mercy of tides and storms, or of the peculiar culture of the merchant vessel. The sailor: outcast to polite society, defiant to all the elements and so set apart by the strangeness of his aspect, roving the seven seas for a wage. The officer: pinched and furious in the isolation he cultivates to increase the aura of his mandate and the effectiveness of his rule.

I cannot say if it was the unfamiliar lurching and pounding motion of the ship, or the vast expanse of sky overhead, the clouds lumbering through the blue plain like giant beasts, or the sailors with their odd dress of tarred breeches and checked gingham, their faces metallic and sun-beaten, or perhaps the incessant creak and strain of the wooden ship against its joinery and nails, but I became seized with the unshakeable conviction that I had stepped into a realm of spirits, so unfamiliar and foreboding did everything around me seem.

Sailors' English is a curious dialect. To the untrained ear it shares something of its intonation with the King's English, but the words and their meanings are compressed and shaken, coming sideways out of whiskered mouths, mixed with profanities and syntax from every tongue the speaker has encountered. Every other utterance is a blasphemous declamation, rendering a statement of fact to sound like a deathbed curse. If you are unfamiliar with their cant, a sailor can look at you squarely in the eye and tell you he's born and bred in London while not a word he utters comes close to comprehension.

A ship upon the open ocean is a world unto itself. Suspended in the watery medium by its physical properties it is as a seedpod built with human hands, cast to float upon the desolate wastes with naught but a crew and a captain and the common work before them. The isolation from the company of society becomes complete for those who walk upon that deck, relying on the firm construction of the hull to separate the human tribe from the salty current. The law of judge and parliament is reduced to its pale representative, the captain, whose rule is tested daily by the respect of the sailors he commands, for a sailor's love of authority is a withered and desiccated fruit. A ship is a tool maneuvered through the field of stars at night and the moody sky by day, a brittle and waterlogged vessel thrown into blusters and tempests that probe every seam to bursting and pull every nail by its head, taking the measure of each sailor aboard. It is a prosthesis that increases the range of humanity; the body on its own in the wastes of the ocean would quickly succumb to the pounding waves.

The first leg of the journey proceeded through the channel between Calais and the ghostly cliffs of Dover, then along the coastal waters of the provinces of France, skirting the jutting peninsulas of Normandy and then Brittany. As the sloop crossed the Bay of Biscay the intemperate weather there produced a squall. A flapping whistle grew to a quick roar and tore off some rigging, causing a delay of several days, for although the damage was slight the repairs were complicated. The day after the squall I was confined to my quarters. Unaccustomed to the motion of a storm upon the sea, I was taken by a violent sensitivity to the slightest roll of the ship; above my own retching complaint I could hear Captain Bellamy upon the deck raging at the sailors as they went about the repairs, cursing them for being slow-moving, for being shadowy skulkers. Throughout the day I heard the lazy slap of his cudgel falling upon the shoulders of any man who ventured within reach of his extended arm.

The first serious injury that I attended on the Royal Fortune was none other than Shelly the carpenter, not nearly as handsome though neither as fierce as reported in the accounts I have read. The occupation of the ship's carpenter is a specialized one, the importance of which cannot be underestimated in a floating world composed entirely of wood, and it is an occupation that bears special dangers. The hard use of the ship occasions constant and unceasing repair, making the carpenter's job one that is never complete, for he is charged with the maintenance of a thing that is always near the point of dissolution. Injuries are frequent and bloody, occasioned by the combination of sharp hand tools with the constant pitch and roll of the ship.

Shelly was mending a balustrade smashed by a barrel that outed its stays during the squall when his chisel slipped and stabbed into the flesh of his thigh. It jumped and quivered with the twitch of the offended muscle as he clenched his jaw so as not to cry out and risk hard words from his shipmates. Eager to prove my worth, I rushed to attend him on the deck, where I removed the blade from his leg and staunched the blood with a clean rag I carried with me for just such an occasion. I called out for help in carrying the injured carpenter down to my quarters where I could sew the wound shut, only to have Captain Bellamy deny my request with a reedy snarl.

"No, Surgeon, you will take him down yourself. You are hired to take care of such things so that they need not interrupt the duties of the crew."

I put the carpenter's arm over my shoulder and took him down the stairs with his leg still hobbled and dripping blood. I could see Shelly was sullen as I laid him on the little cot in my cabin.

"Please just hold the bandage while I open my kit," I said awkwardly as I turned to find the needle and thread for stitching up his wound.

"You must know that I bear your person no ill will,

Surgeon; it is rather the captain against whom I hold a claim," said Shelly. Perhaps he saw that I was intimidated by the angry set of his jaw. "I've not before had the misfortune of sailing with this bastard Bellamy, and after this cursed round I never will again."

Shelly told me he had been born to a Quaker family in the hills of Pennsylvania, where he was perfectly content with the clang of the scythe on the stony fields as he cut the straw in late summer. But he went down to Philadelphia on apprenticeship and there was taken off the streets against his will by a press gang of navy men looking for able bodies to serve in the last days of the Spanish War. Since then it was the seafaring life that called him. When I met him, he was thirteen years upon the sea.

"It's not a bad life," he said. "It's that the yoke grows heavy when it's not handled well."

After the completion of repairs, the Royal Fortune sailed on to the port of Lisbon, where Columbus and da Gama once launched their fleets with ribbons upon the bowsprits. The lights of the Ribeira Palace gleamed at our nighttime approach and in the morning I saw the crimson tile and sparkle of that great city spreading out around us. After a week in the port spent taking on supplies and waiting for favorable winds, the Royal Fortune unfurled its sail towards

the Canary Isles, there to seek the sheet of steel-grey water
that marks the strong westward current.

✳

Within days of departure from Lisbon, the entire crew
was taken terribly ill—the hold full of sailors moaning
at the fearsome turning of their guts, their brows burning with raging fevers, insides turned to a bloody water,
bellies hard and rumbling as if filled with hives of furious
creatures. I did my best to comfort the stricken men, but
in such cases there is little to be done besides ensure that
the sufferer has liquid to replace what spews out of him.
The sailors cursed Bellamy between bouts of sickness, and
the close air of their quarters quickly became overpowering, forcing those with enough strength to drag their sore
bodies above to sleep on the deck, where their bubble and
spew was washed down with buckets of seawater in the
morning.

"You aiming to make a name for yourself, Surgeon?"
the Hindu sailor asked me as I offered him a cup of water
and a compress for his fever. (When I asked him his name
he told me it was Tharinda.)

"Not exactly, but I have newly completed my studies to
be a surgeon and am seeking to increase the range of my
practical experience before returning to London to start my
own practice."

Tharinda looked at me narrow-eyed as I spoke. "I'll tell you this, Surgeon, and take it as you like: the ship's command maintains that by taking on a surgeon less sailors are required, and so there's more gold for the owners and shareholders. They drive the tars they have to work harder and faster, figuring an injury takes less time to heal when properly attended. A surgeon aboard means longer shifts, an excuse to push us tars back to work no matter the complaint."

Tharinda grimaced as his guts bubbled and squirmed beneath my palms. Although he did not refuse my ministrations, I came to understand that my posting aboard the Royal Fortune was not entirely welcome to the sailors, as it augured a deterioration of the conditions of their work.

I felt it was my duty to make some inquiry as to the source of the sailors' illness, and in interviewing the cook discovered that some of the provisions provided to the common sailors were rotten, several barrels of meat being infested with worms that turned the salt pork into a fetid, greyish mass. There were larvae visible to the eye as the meat was spooned out of the barrel to be added to the stew. The cook became indignant as he told me how he had protested against serving such spoiled fare, rightly fearing that the crew might hold him to account when they came down sick;

he maintained that Captain Bellamy insisted the spoiled meat be served.

"So that the dogs would get their guts in order, he told me!" said the cook.

Captain Bellamy did not fear any inconvenience to his person, as the victuals prepared for officers were of a different order and supply than those prepared for the crew. After our conversation the cook surreptitiously flung that rotten meat off the deck of the ship, shoveling the stinking flesh out to be nibbled by the darting fish that made their home in the shadow of the ship.

When a ship crawls within sight of a coastline it is easy enough to follow the familiar relief of land on the horizon, the ridges and jutting peninsulas, the great bays, the undulations of the shore, the mountain peak rising blue in the distance. A good pilot's chart—drawn and redrawn by successive navigators, carefully bundled in a sheaf of maps and parchment—will show the hidden geography below the surface of the ocean, the rocky outcrops and sandy shoals that could run the ship aground or put a hole in the hull. But even within familiar seas, traveled and mapped for generations, uncharted hazards can arise: shallows and sandbars that move with the shifting of the sea-bed, boulders wrenched and tossed in a great storm, reefs that are invisible at high tide and escape the record.

Mr. Alexander was the second mate, come up through the hawsehole, as they say of a sailor who becomes an officer after having begun his career as a simple tar. He explained that he was not bred to command but was given over to the roving life and would walk the path that was made for him. His burly form was covered with a leathery skin whose undulating tattoos spoke of many years at sea. He bore a scar on his cheek that was only visible when he trimmed his reddish beard; he said there was a splinter lodged there from when a Dutch cannon ball exploded across the deck in the years when he wore the blue woolens of a navy man. Mr. Alexander explained to me the principles of navigation, the division of the earth by the latitude of the angle north or south of the equator, the measurement of distance traveled by triangulation with the glinting stars above. I saw him fix the position of the stars with his sextant, referring to his tables to record the position of the ship. He was great company. I sat with him on many a cool and calm night while he maintained the course of the ship, as the mantle of heavenly bodies overhead glistened, reflected in the ruffles of the ocean that spread its skirt as far as the eye could see.

✳

It was mid-afternoon on the fourth day after the Royal Fortune had begun the crossing of the wide Atlantic that

a sharp and cold wind rose up off the starboard bow, while
in the distance a turbulence of dark clouds was spotted and
the sailors barked to one another like a pack of dogs warning of an intruder.

The sailors scrambled to prepare against the threat
of the looming cloud bank, moving below deck whatever
could be hauled and tying down the rest, bringing in and
fastening the sails, checking all the blocking. Within the
hour sharp needles of rain began to fall and the wind blew
a low howl. Any person who has experienced it can tell you
that the worst storm on land is a lamb compared to even a
mild squall upon the sea. By evening the eye of the tempest
passed over us with great force. The ship bobbed on waves
twice its height and plunged into valleys where the frothy
walls surrounding it loomed to terrifying effect; the pelt of
rain came down in a wash and the waves coursed over the
deck.

The men fought sharp blasts of wind as Bellamy stood
among them in an anxious state, cursing and shouting
commands. A section of the rigging came undone, leaving
the sail slapping violently and the yardarm swinging wildly,
threatening everyone in its path. Bellamy asked about the
boy whose duty it was to scuttle up the masts and was told
the deckhand lay shivering in the hold. He had been sickly
since eating the corrupted feed and was down again with
the squirts. Bellamy was overcome with rage, the bulging

veins of his neck visible in the strange half-darkness of the storm. He fought his way across the deck, leaning into the wind, and pushed into the hold to emerge moments later with the young seaman in tow: bleeding from a wound at his head, his eyes filmy and disoriented, the fever in them visible even from a distance.

Bellamy hauled the deckhand to the mast, commanding him to climb up and untangle the rigging. As soon as Bellamy released his hold the boy fell to the deck in a waterlogged heap. The captain cursed again, his face twisted, and began to pour blows on the boy with his fists.

The young sailor shook as he hauled himself up the mast while the winds gusted and blew icy rain at him from all angles. I was certain he would be blown away from the ship and lost forever to the oblivion of the deep. With great effort he cut loose the knotted bunches of rope, then was blown into the falling sail. After he tumbled onto the deck I made my way over to him and struggled to carry him back to the hold, to see if I might restore some semblance of life.

It was then that I acquired an assistant and apprentice. Jeremiah adopted me after I dragged him down from the deck to patch him up. Afterwards I argued with Bellamy for the injured deckhand to be granted a day's bed rest, so that he could recover from his wounds. Thereafter, although Bellamy insisted that Jeremiah continue to perform his assigned duties on deck, the moment he was finished he would accompany me on my rounds and was an invaluable assistant in my daily practice of repairing the wounds and contusions of rough work and regular disciplinary beatings administered by the captain and first mate. Jeremiah was fourteen years old, he said, and a man; he was hard about the eyes but the softness of his cheek spoke otherwise.

Jeremiah demonstrated a keen interest in the mechanics of the body, so I showed him the rudiments of medicine. He observed the stitching of minor wounds and assisted as I prepared poultices to ease sunburn, bruises, and sore muscles. One evening a tar came to us with his arm jutting at an odd angle after being violently displaced by a line that snapped with a sudden gust of wind. The tar sat silently, his face washed with quiet tears of pain, as I showed Jeremiah the position of the hands required for yanking the disjointed arm back into its socket.

Jeremiah told me that the director of the poorhouse where he had spent his childhood had sold him for a pittance to serve as an apprentice on the Royal Fortune. He was not contracted to receive a wage at any point during the voyage—what little pay he might have received went to the director of the poorhouse, who kept himself in the wine and silk kerchiefs that he favored by selling the services of his charges. Jeremiah explained that he nevertheless hoped to become surefooted on a ship, so that he could return to London having earned the bowlegged walk that distinguishes a man of the sea and gives a sailor the privilege of swaggering up to the docks of Wapping, Bristol, or Liverpool and selling his precious labor to the highest bidder.

✴

Captain Bellamy had made his career at sea. He served in the Navy in times of war and in the merchant marine when there was money to be had. As surgeon I took my meals with Bellamy and the first mate, a privilege that Alexander refused, preferring to go to mess with the common tars. When drunk, Bellamy would occasionally break up the misery of dinner with tales of exotic locales, showing us the dots he had put on his arm in a fishing village in Borneo or recounting the horrors of working the slaving ships where half the crew died of disease, their bodies tipped over the side of the ship at night to hide the deaths from the slaves crammed in the hold, sharks trailing the lee of the ship waiting for a fresh corpse. His storytelling induced an atmosphere of easy joviality that caused me to mistake my place and ask a question that had been plaguing me.

"Why is it, sir, that you use the men so?"

Bellamy looked at me curiously when I finished my question, rolling down his sleeves as he did, indicating an end to the informal atmosphere that had prevailed at the table. I was about to apologize for my presumptuousness when the captain began to speak, his rough voice crackling in his throat.

"I see that you have little experience in the world, Surgeon, for you to question me around my treatment of the crew. Listen to me now, and listen well, for after this night to question me again will put you in the brig where you can engage the bilge rats in your speculations.

"Who do you think, gentle soul, harvests the tea that you drink, clearing hillsides and planting bushes in the tropical heat? Who spins the cotton that you wear, who plants it and harvests those bolls from their spiny twig? Who weaves the linens from the oily flax? Who sows the corn that makes your bread? It is the bitter threat of hunger or the sharp bite of a whip that puts the food at your table and the clothing on your back. And how is all that vital produce dispersed throughout the world? You think it is brought on the wings of carrier pigeons carting hogsheads as they might a message tied to their wrinkly feet? No, Surgeon, it is through the strain of men's muscles across the endless deep, through storms that echo the apocalypse. The crew you sympathize with is on this ship to receive a wage so that they may continue to eat. Remember, Surgeon—" Bellamy ended his speech shaking his finger at me, his puffy face reddened "—that as I am captain, this ship is my realm. Out here on the open ocean the very blood that pulses in your veins and the resilience of each of your sinews is mine."

SEA MONSTER; OR, A CONFESSION
As told to the Ordinary of Marshalsea Prison
in the course of his regular ministry

I hear you have been the ordinary here since the doomed exploits of Captain Kidd came to their final reckoning, and I imagine that you stand outside my cell thirsty to receive yet another confession to mark in your journal of good deeds. Do you haunt the cells of 3all the prisoners here in Marshalsea, offering the swaddle of a Christian hereafter to those already condemned to settle their accounts among the worms? If I were to tell a convincing tale of moral disaster and repentance, perhaps you might publish an account of my sin and regret? Distribute it at the public houses to warn others away from my hard fate? While I am certainly able to admit fault, and even guilt where guilt may lie, I am sorry to tell you that I cannot offer you a confession to crimes of piracy, though this infernal purgatory sometimes makes me almost crave the noose, even if it were to mean laying claim to the wildest crimes.

No, it is a more ephemeral sort of guilt that I suffer, a sense of personal failure that has dogged me ever since I witnessed the destruction of my family as a young lad. A haunting cloud of responsibility has been my companion ever since, riding my shoulder and whispering in my ear, making me finally a most sensitive creature, in a constant state of fear. Truly it is a horror, but likely not the one you hope to hear of as I fall on my knees to offer supplication and penance.

A former cellmate of mine told me tales of the press yard at Newgate, where the jailers squeeze confession from those accused of piracy like juice from a ripe fruit: the offender is laid out in the yard, his limbs splayed and secured by means of chains staked into the ground. Plates of lead are piled on his abdomen day by day as he is taunted there, until his lungs are so compressed that he can barely squeeze in a breath and his organs are squashed like jelly in a bag; he must confess or die of a burst spleen. If the accused person chooses the former, well, I suppose in finding himself before the pearly gates he might say: "I was a bad man, a whore, a fiendish child—but I did repent before I died, so let me now in to the company of the right livers."

How was it with Captain Kidd? He must have challenged you when you were still a young man, your collar crisp and fresh as you pled with him to admit the accusation: that he murdered the gunner on his ship in a fit of pique. Of course, Captain Kidd laid the blame on his crew, their mutinous and scheming ways—he was not the first captain to blame things upon the very men he misused and certainly will not be the last, for I suspect there is some inherent poison in the possession of authority that grievously tempts a person to abuse those who stand below him.

Looking at the purse of your lips as you listen, I imagine that you were quite earnest in battling Kidd's drunken protestations of innocence, and that when the gallows broke, leaving him alive on his knees in the dirt, you saw an opportunity to redouble your appeals. It must have felt a great victory when at that last moment he said the words you had awaited: "I am sorry I did it."

I heard of Kidd when I was still a child, long before I ever saw the white-capped waves of the sea. His crimes and bitter confession were published on broadsheet and hung on posts at the street corners. His body swung gibbeted over the Thames for years thereafter, the jaws of his skull chattering in a high wind.

❋

A man after your own heart, Captain Bellamy was also

concerned for the immortal souls of the sailors under his command.

"With good discipline and a little instruction these men might be put on the path of righteousness," he used to mutter. He thought himself endowed with a special gift for understanding and transmitting the teachings of the Church of England.

Bellamy declared a Sunday service aboard ship. In fair weather he would command the shifting crew of sailors to gather on the deck; the air whistled with their sighs as he read from the Bible for their edification. He always picked a passage at random and spoke in a booming voice for no more than a few minutes; the reading proceeded from the beginning of a page to its end regardless of where it fell in the chapter or the narrative—as if the words themselves contained a power that required no discernible structure or moral to work its magic.

At the beginning of the voyage of the Royal Fortune, Captain Bellamy instituted a market day on Friday of every week. On that day he settled accounts for violations of the ship's rules, which seemed to me as arbitrary and capricious as the wind. He set it for a Friday to ensure that the corrected sailors had a day to recover from their bloody stripes, that they might remain receptive to the Sunday homily.

The disciplining was largely for minor infractions. The first mate, Peter Finch, would lay into the condemned with a length of knotted rope gone tough and leathery with time, beating him good and hard about the back and shoulders. The crewman toward whom Finch bore some personal animosity would find the rope curling around his shoulder to blacken his eye.

Once I had to set a man's nose after market day. It was Tharinda the Hindu, punished for falling asleep on watch in that quietest hour before the sun rises. Yes, his nose was broke for that, but he was a hard man; though small and wiry, Tharinda maintained his calm and the faintest trace of a smirk as the first mate lay into him. As I set his nose and plugged his nostrils to stop the bleeding, I was surprised when he said that this was not the cruelest usage he had received. He bragged that he had served on voyages where the entire crew completed the terms of their service blackened and hobbling from their beatings, like a colony of lepers set afloat upon the sea.

I found it most disturbing to hear the captain's hissing rants, for in the course of the beatings he had the habit of working himself into a froth: "Boy, do not force me further, for the next time you fail me I will turn you inside out and have your liver on a plate, I will splay you out like a side of beef and feed your eyeballs to the gulls, I will trim the sail

with the yards of your intestines, make a soup of your bones
and invite the bilge rats to sup on it. Fail me not, or you will
suffer things that will make you beg for a bed at the bottom
of the sea, where the crabs will have at you, pulling at your
prick with their claws and feeding on your stilled heart."
Bellamy would go on with his foul whispering for the duration of the beating, the sailor managing as best he could to
hold his tongue all the while, although many were brought
to moaning and complaint.

✻

I had expected that crossing the Atlantic would reveal an
endless sterile expanse and was surprised to find in those
watery wastes a wild proliferation of life not subject to the
civilizing hand of man. Out in the deepest sea there are pods
of great leatherback turtles asleep upon the waves; countless
fish that cluster and disperse in great schools; porpoises that
swim one behind the other like hounds chasing a stag, leaping and chortling along the sides of the ship. On a moonlit
night it is possible to spot great ghostly fluthers of jellyfish
bobbing just below the surface of the sea. There are *bonito*,
Spanish mackerel, and albacore, the albacore being most
favored by the sailors for their excellent meat; at all times of
day a fishing line trails behind the ship, as the sailors hope
to supplement their paltry provisions with a cauldron of fish
stew. The shark is an enemy to sailors, since it is known to

feast upon the dead committed to burial at sea, so when sailors catch a shark on the line they treat it with marked cruelty. After wrestling the shark onto the deck, they put out its eyes, and then they push the blinded creature back into the sea.

One morning, soon after the peaks of the Canary Isles had disappeared behind the horizon, I was surprised to observe a pair of whale-fish, a mother and her calf. Their graceful shadows slid through the waves barely a stone's throw from the ship. I heard their exhalations—they were so close—and felt a fine spray as they made ready to submerge. Alexander sidled up next to me and broke my spell of wonderment with his gravelly voice.

"It may seem unlikely, but there was a time when the whale-fish gathered here by the thousands," he said, sideways.

In contemplating the retreat of that great and wondrous pair of whale-fish, I replied that I could not conceive of such a number of them gathered in one place.

"When I was young, I sailed on a ship that also visited this part of the world." He waved his hand at the bluish horizon. "In a certain season the ocean here was filled as far the eye could see by great schools of whale-fish, their shadows sliding all around the ship. I had occasion to meet the intelligence of one of them, who broke the surface with her eye staring straight into mine, and I still maintain that

I saw an otherworldly light in that limpid gaze. They would leap, spewing great jets of water, their enormous bodies flying full into the air, then splash happily down, threatening to capsize any vessel that got too close. I will tell you that as a young man peering upon those fish I was brought to tears by the happiness of their play; I never would have thought that those great beasts would cavort like puppies amongst schooners doing the dour business of men."

"Do we now come upon them in the wrong season?" I asked.

"No," said Alexander, "I have passed this way in many seasons for many years, and it seems the population of whale-fish in these parts has dwindled to the point of disappearance, like those islands in our wake have just done.

"It was no secret that the whale-fish liked to converge here to perform their happy ritual, and men find great value in hunting them. One may eat whale meat—it has a fatty flavor, but is rich enough—more important, though, is the whale oil used to make a smoky beam that penetrates deep into the darkness of the night. At first it was only the Basques who came to catch whales here. But soon whale fishermen of all languages arrived with the spear thrust that stills all activity with the sharpness of its argument. At one time there were so many ships that in approaching this bit of ocean under cover of night, you would see a great constellation of bobbing lights upon the sea, fires burning

SEA MONSTER

round the clock to render the fat to oil, the sea churning with long and bloody carcasses. You are lucky to have spied that pair; I thought that in these seas those creatures were long extinct."

※

It was Aristotle, intoxicated by the breadth of Greek wisdom, who started the practice of taxonomy: the cataloguing of all living things, taming the efflorescence of form and function through the tracing of relation as indicated by the shape of leaves, the curve of stamens, the rippling of bark, the curl of ears, the coarseness of hair, or the sharpness of canines. It seems that for men all things must always be arranged in a hierarchy, with God impassive at the top, prim-mouthed, and below him the human being and his misshapen brothers, the other anthropomorpha: the Patagonian dwarf; the wolf-boy whose hairy form haunts the barns of countless Teutonic peasants; the Himalayan giant who croons behind the snowdrifts.

Sir Francis Bacon called for a catalogue of the entire contents of the planet, a sprawling library of illustrations ordered by attributes, geographical ranges, and habits, with dried specimens and cross sections arrayed in a vast and universal cabinet. Bacon hoped that each vessel serving the expansion of the British Empire would carry with it a naturalist to collect samples of seed pods, pressed flowers, and skeletal remains, and to bring these back to one cavernous repository—thus resolving the fog of multiplicity into sharp and discrete categories.

Do you think it possible that the economy of nature could be so prone to imbalance that a species of whale-fish could actually disappear? That the last mother of them could be cut to pieces so her blubber might be separated from her flesh and scraped into barrels, as the last whale-calf wanders off forlorn to end its days among the sharks and other wolves of the sea? There are those who assert it is an insult to accuse Nature of having links in her great chain that are so weak as to be broken; these men claim that anecdotal reports of the disappearance of certain creatures do not prove them gone once and for all. Yet it seems to me that even within the tangled web of life there is change: tidal shifts and flows, the possibility of disappearance—as well, perhaps, as the emergence of new expressions of nature. The destruction of a known form can only be possible in an order where the emergence of the newly formed and unexpected is also possible, and so the project of creation and annihilation must remain forever incomplete.

After several weeks of sailing in the direction of the West Indies it became apparent that the ship was off course. Days were lost to long tacks north or south in an attempt to right the trajectory. I spoke on it with Alexander one night, when the cloak of stars was so thick it seemed to press down upon us.

"We're off course," he said, his tone both resigned and playful. "Every night I have to make corrections. I'll show you the logs—you'll see the gaps on the pages, the places where the captain or the first mate fell asleep or lost interest."

Alexander seemed strangely unperturbed by floating without direction. The crew, however, grew surly and agitated. They were beginning to realize that their commanders used them with casual cruelty, yet did not demonstrate the competence by which authority justifies itself. I noticed Bellamy and Finch arguing with Alexander as to who merited the blame for our drifting, a heated exchange that ended with curses when Alexander threw the logbook on the floor and stormed out of the captain's cabin.

Although the benefit of retrospect does allow me to pick out certain signs and indications, at the time I did not recognize any politicking among the crew of the Royal Fortune—no portent of the storm that was to come. I did notice that Shelly had taken on an earnest air, and I remember frequently happening upon him in sincere and discreet conversation with other members of the crew— sitting quiet in little clutches on great nests of bundled rope, or in between the looming cargo in the hold, or on the stairs—but I was an innocent to shipboard life and could not read the currents that coursed between the men, any more than I could read the ones that ran below the surface of the ocean. I could not decipher the implications of those stolen moments.

Bellamy insisted that his officers maintain strict social isolation from the crew, who naturally reciprocated the disdain that was offered them. As surgeon, I was regarded as an officer by the sailors, and so I was not privy to the content of their dealings, apart from what little gossip I could glean from Jeremiah. Bellamy explained that the social order he imposed was necessary to ensure that no sympathy would creep into his business of giving commands—so that he might hold the sailors to an account as final as the sear of a mare's flesh when she is branded against all other owners. Alexander paid these strictures no mind at all, choosing instead to freely mix among the crew as he saw fit. When the captain took him to task for his insubordination with a gnashing of teeth and barbed threats, Alexander stood his ground, confident in the indispensability of his skills to the success of the voyage.

I did notice that the gaming and drinking that was regular on nights when the wind was quiet and steady took on a more somber aspect. The sailors' low conversation floated on the wind—but how was I to know it was the murmur of Defiance as she heaved the dirt from atop her grave? Jeremiah did seem pregnant with some story he would not communicate, but I figured him shaded by the gathering gloom that enveloped the ship. He was still affectionate with me and attentive to the duties of physician's assistant that he had assumed, which Bellamy grudgingly allowed, saying, "That boy is no sail monkey anyways; a rather weak and unbalanced specimen, barely suited to scrubbing the deck."

✳

We were thirty-five days away from the last sight of land when the monster was spotted. By that time the conditions aboard the Royal Fortune had greatly deteriorated. Bellamy was taken nearly every day by a devilish mood. As if in resistance to the sharpening of his demands, the sailors grew ever more lackadaisical in the execution of their duties. The provisions had run low; fresh water was on ration.

Roger Eaves was a common sailor with whom I had become well acquainted. As he was both a clumsy man and insubordinate by nature, I tended often to the injuries he sustained. It was just past the start of the morning shift when this Eaves let loose a cry.

"Look, that is no fish," he wailed. "Look at that evil shape—I tell you it is a serpent trailing this accursed ship, the source of all our misfortune."

The sailors on deck rushed over to see a strange apparition wriggling in the distance before slipping beneath the surface of the water without a splash. I saw its outline myself and can attest that it did not look like any other creature I had seen in my months upon the sea. Captain Bellamy shouted down from the forecastle that it was nothing: a play of light upon the water; a school of fish or some other nonsense.

"Eaves, you fool, I'll not have you distracting the crew with your nonsense. Back to your post, you bugger, or I'll stripe your back again!"

Eaves muttered under his breath but went back to his post, where the other sailors stopped by to question him about what he had seen. Later, when the men took their supper, Eaves could be heard describing the creature in increasingly fantastic terms.

After the day when Eaves spotted the sea monster, I grew obsessed with watching the horizon of bobbing waves to see if I could also catch sight of the creature. I had begun to realize that attending to the minor injuries of the crew would not provide me with the surgical experience I needed to make my career, and in my desperation became convinced that it would serve to consolidate my professional credentials if I could record an observation of a sea serpent, a species that had never before been fully accounted in the literature. I began to keep my notebook handy so I might capture a description of the creature should it reappear, as I devoted countless hours to gazing into the distance.

I thought myself well prepared to catalogue such a being, as prior to the voyage I had reviewed the *Historia animalium* specifically to familiarize myself with the order of sea monsters: denizens of the unsearchable depths, who confound and perturb the natural order of things. I had taken an interest in natural history since long before the days when I sketched out the anatomy of the creatures I dismembered in the butcher shop. As a child, I had learned the names of all the songbirds that adorn the English countryside in the summer months, chirping in the eaves of the trees amid bright flashes of color. Yes, once I could name each and every one; but alas, long years have dulled my recollections of the fluttering of wings.

As I kept my vigil on the deck, Shelly approached me and cast a curious glance at the notebook I held out expectantly, its blank sheets flapping in the breeze. "Why do you keep your eyes on the horizon, Surgeon? There's not enough here on the ship to keep you occupied?"

"I am looking for the sea serpent that Eaves spotted the other day. Perhaps the creature menaces us from across the expanse, seeing in our passage some opportunity we cannot fathom. If it does appear again, I wish to record its attributes," I said, attempting to convey the seriousness of my purpose.

"Well, Surgeon," said Shelly, "I do hope you spy the creature; but if it is menace that concerns you, I think the danger may be closer than you know."

I turned, curious at the note of disdain and swagger in his voice, but he was already departing. As I returned to my vigil at the balustrade I saw beneath the wake of the ship a shadow of great and commanding shape.

"Sea monster!" I cried out involuntarily, and was immediately embarrassed, but the men rushed quickly to my side—Eaves at their head, yelling his vindication.

"I knew it! I seen the bastard now some days ago, and here he is again, waiting on us, haunting this boat!"

The men clustered around me at the starboard as the shadow passed beneath us; they sent up a great clamor and commotion until Bellamy stalked out of his cabin shouting at them to return to work. There it was, still—the shadow passed under the boat; finally the head of that serpent lifted itself—now eighty yards or more away, and so huge that it could be judged to reach as high as the masthead. The murk of its body spreading below the water had as much bulk as the ship, and was accompanied by a stench of ammonia that overpowered the clean salt of the ocean, causing the sailors to double over retching as they recoiled in fear.

The creature had a greyish, mottled skin, and a tooth protruded with a fearsome sharpness from within its folds. Around it there was a ruffle of coils that rippled with unpleasant spasms. The men groaned at the darkness of its maw before the monster turned and dipped quietly below the water, finally disappearing with a geyser of spray and leaving a silence that was broken only when Eaves himself said, "You see there, you bastards; you see there, Bellamy—God damn you if you put stripes upon me for telling tales now, you son of a whore, for there's the creature itself, and this shipment is surely doomed."

The Book of Nature; or, an Infernal Combination

As told to an investigator of the West Indian Merchants' Association

A full month of hell followed the day on which we sighted the sea monster. Her apparition went on haunting the ship, the serpentine form slithering into the dreams of the crew as they swung and turned in their canvas hammocks. Yet apart from this general sense of unease and dread, there was no warning of the fateful day of rebellion, which came as the ship heaved upon the waves not more than a week from the island of Jamaica.

It was a market day, when Bellamy and Finch would settle accounts for infractions they had recorded against the sailors in the course of the previous week. There was a chilling tableau set up on the deck: the sailor to be flogged lying over the barrel; the first mate standing with his arm raised to the sky, ready to strike. On that day it was a different account that would be settled. Shouting and taunts began to ring in the air as Finch drew his arm back to begin the flogging. When Captain Bellamy turned to address the jeering crew, he gripped his gnarled cudgel fiercely. But that knot of oak did not taste the kiss of a split cheek, for as Bellamy turned, Shelly stepped forward against his raised hand. I did not see the blade, but in a swift stroke he lopped off the bottom of Bellamy's earlobe, which fell to the deck with a faint plop as a momentary silence fell.

No great violence was visited upon Bellamy and Finch, though they surely feared for their lives as the crew beat them about the deck. There was yet more cutting and blood when Roger Eaves took the captain's drinking glasses from the stateroom and flung them at him, one after another. Captain Bellamy was not spry; the heave of the ship knocked him off balance as he dodged. He cried out when broken bits of glass drove into his hand.

I can attest that the mutineers did not then take Bellamy and cut his belly open and pull out his knotted entrails and nail them to the mast. They did not tie Finch to the mast and have at him with hot needles until he was reduced to a translucent and bloody mass, quivering on the deck like a beached and palpitating jellyfish. Both of them were much abused, yes, but not murdered. The sailors had at them with their fists and they said humiliating things, and Eaves even pissed on Finch when he was bound and helpless, but there was no killing.

I will swear to any power that the last that I saw of Bellamy and Finch was the two of them huddled forlorn in the bottom of a rowboat, set off into a sea-lane where another merchant ship could come along to find them. After all the poking and bloodletting had come to an end, the mutineers were sated in the expression of their rage, and I was given permission to bandage both Bellamy and Finch before they were set adrift, so I can attest that they were well sutured. If they survived, you may interrogate them; I am sure they will support my testimony. It is cruel but true to say that they struck a rather comic figure, the two of them wrapped up stiff with bandages as they struggled with the oars. The cook laughed and danced and cursed them both. Eaves whistled a tune that barely drowned out Finch's desperate pleadings as they drifted away.

❋

As evening lowered its indigo veil, the mutineers slacked the sails and arrayed themselves in a great circle, convening what I thought the strangest council ever held. To guide their deliberations, the men chose Samuel Parsons, the aged cook whose knotted joints and gnarled face spoke of a long and arduous life at sea. Each man was then given the chance to speak his mind—even Jeremiah, who was the youngest and least experienced among them. Jeremiah did not speak much, however, since he was enthralled by the adventure that had overtaken him, stricken dumb by his excitement.

It was quickly decided that there were only two possible choices: for the mutineers to make for the nearest Crown port and throw themselves upon the mercy of the Admiralty Court—pleading their mutiny as justified in the face of ill-usage by Bellamy and Finch—or for them to elect the course of piracy, thus forming a conspiracy against the tyranny of commerce in an attempt to make their fortune.

Alexander and I were excluded from the discussion, as we were members of the officer class and our opinions of no account. We were held so that we would continue the performance of our essential duties, myself to repair insults against the flesh and Alexander to chart a course by the stars as the Royal Fortune made whatever journey her new gang of masters should choose. I admit I was glad not to end my days in a leaky rowboat circled by sharks and other predators of the sea. Alexander was glad as well, but less out of concern for his own safety, I think, and more out of a certain sympathy for the mutineers. Alexander and I stood to one side, leaning upon the balustrade, observing the debate as intently as if we were in Parliament watching the passage of some great and consequential law.

I can tell you that there was serious consideration of the mutineers submitting themselves to the judgment of the Admiralty Court. Thomas Jones was the strongest advocate of this course. Jones was a son of the Americas; he once told me his mother was an Indian of Massachusetts, who wandered out of her village as a girl after her people were struck down by a plague. Her parents and siblings had gone blue and stiff and swollen with decay before she tore herself from their sides. She made her way to Boston, where she married an Englishman who sought his fortune in the fur trade and felt the best treatment for a half-caste son was a firm hand with the switch. On the deck that night, in his smoky baritone, Thomas Jones argued that behind the Court's pretense of neutrality it was commercial interests that held sway, and that if the mutineers were to offer their precious cargo in exchange for the Court's consideration, they might have the means to negotiate their freedom.

"To form a combination for the purpose of piracy might surely hold rewards," he said, "but don't forget it brings penalties as well. The world is growing smaller by the day, and the interests of commerce more consolidated with the rattle of each coin that drops into the coffers of the Bank of England. The age of flagrant defiance is gone down as the range of the Admiralty's cannon-shot goes up. While

we might justly dream of the riches and liberty that have so
far been denied us, we must also consider the hard reality,
which includes the possibility of a fatal drop after a long
walk, our necks cracked at the end of a rope."

Roger Eaves responded in a roundabout way: "I once
met a beggar who was a most pitiful creature, sunken cheeks,
hardly any flesh on his bones—holding out a broken hand
from between his rags in a stinking alleyway of Wapping.
When I asked him what had broke him so, he told me he
had been a sailor until wrongly charged with petty theft."

Eaves followed with tales of the conditions of imprison-
ment found in the jails of the West Indies: the long nights
in the cells where there are creatures that feast upon a pris-
oner until he is driven mad, his body a trough to parasites
and blood-drinkers. The lash is applied with artful cruelty
for the slightest infraction, and terrible diseases ravage the
precincts of a naval prison like a spring rain, innocent and
guilty alike suffering the eruption of their vitals, a horrible
spewing from fore and aft, the flesh peeling off them in strips,
boils erupting on their tongues. It was there, in fact, that the
beggar was broken, accused of stealing a few candles from
the captain of his ship. He was found innocent when the
candles were discovered somewhere no one had thought to
look, but only after his health was robbed from him.

"Those being the conditions of confinement," Eaves
continued, cackling as he said it, "if a mutineer is found

innocent and does not end his days upon the gallows, he nevertheless leaves his trial a broken man."

The assembled sailors grew serious and quiet.

"Under these conditions what justice could we possibly hope for?" asked Shelly, advocating a path of permanent rebellion. "Can we do naught but careen between the madness of Captain Bellamy and the partial and biased justice of the Admiralty, which does not serve interests of sailors but rather is exclusive to the interests of their employers? The owners of these shipping ventures accumulate in steady increment clinking mountains of gold that serve to make brilliant the spires and country estates of innumerable aristocrats, all while we sailors remain poor and miserable devoting our lives to a cruel and capricious occupation. We are reliant on the whims of captain and employer to provide a pittance of a wage, drowning our sorrow in bitterness and competition for the meager scraps afforded us. Why continue to play our part, waiting until the end of days, when the trumpets sound, for happiness and well-being? I charge you, let us seize what is before us and live at our own measure and by our own rule."

Then Shelly went down into the hold and brought up a bundle of goods and a barrel of port, his shoulders heaving with the effort. He threw them upon the deck, and, using a long knife to cut the stays on the package, he spilled forth a sumptuous collection of the most delicate textiles. Using an axe, he made a quick hole in the barrel as well, pouring the finest Madeira port upon the deck until the men put their saucers to it and had a drink.

It was deep in the night before the vote was made, though when it was called it was quick work, for there was no dissent. It would be piracy. Shelly was elected captain in matters of war and negotiation, after Eaves gave him a resounding endorsement—"Being a carpenter, if any man could keep this ship afloat, it's he, and should he be so saucy as to exceed his prescription, then down with him!"—to which the assembled mutineers roared. Thomas Jones was elected quartermaster, as his fastidious and even nature inspired trust.

They drew up articles which listed the rules they commonly agreed would govern them: their enterprise would continue until their bounty could apportion each member eight hundred pounds. The shares of each prize were to be divided in strict proportion among the conspirators. Any man who chose to hide a portion of the prize or sought to run away would be marooned or shot. Any man who was maimed would receive a certain reward for his loss, depending on the values placed upon each body part, which they listed out from finger to leg, eyes and ears as well. Any man killed before the venture's end would receive an award to be paid to his kin. Any man who failed to hold his weapons and equipment in good working order at all times would receive lashes upon his back. Lights and candles were to be extinguished at eight o'clock. It went on so: a good many rules for a pirate band, it may seem, but I have heard such is the standard for these infernal combinations.

After each sailor had nodded his assent to the articles as they were read, he made his mark upon the document, and it was tucked away somewhere safe, for next there was drink to be had. They set about finishing the barrel of port and then brought up another, until the morning found them all drunk upon the deck, draped in the bright fabrics that had been shipped from Liverpool to be fashioned into modish gowns for the idle wives of planters.

You ask about the merchants who did truck with the pirates: betrayers among the planter class, who met us in moonlit bays to trade coin for illicit goods. So paid, the pirates could convert their high-seas harvest into gold, welcome at any port and on any high street in the world. I can certainly give you the names of the merchants, describe the silhouettes of their faces, and account the nature and quantity of the goods acquired. I will tell you about their hairy hands and the cloth of their overcoats if you like—if, in return, you might consider lodging a petition with my jailors that I be furnished more pleasant accommodations. I am finding it difficult to sleep for the creaking of my own bones, and one would think a person could grow accustomed to the foul smell here, but that pile of shit in the corner grows with each passing day. These conditions are hardly fit for beasts; I think that I would prefer the supervision of a zookeeper to that of the jailors here.

❄

Once they had decided on the darkling path of robbery upon the high seas, the pirates set a course for the Windward Isles at the southern end of the archipelago of the Antilles, where Alexander told me there were a number of small and uninhabited islets that offered discreet respite for mariners. Shelly and Thomas Jones worked closely with Alexander as he plotted the course, first determining the present position of the Royal Fortune and then, by chart and sextant, determining the desired trajectory, accounting for the prevailing winds. Alexander was not jealous of his knowledge. He shared it freely, encouraging Shelly to make the calculations and showing Mr. Jones the mysteries of the sextant, reviewing their calculations and correcting them where necessary.

It was near a week of avoiding the main shipping lanes before a holler went up. Jeremiah pointed out the silhouette of a lone bird circling in the clear blue sky. When I asked the significance of that winged signpost, Alexander explained that the frigate bird ranges deep into the wastes of the ocean, far from where its nest is made on the rocky coast, making it the first land-dwelling creature that is spotted upon the open ocean: a sure sign throughout the equatorial latitudes that landfall is nigh.

"That bird is something of a bandit," observed Alexander as we stood together on the deck. "He makes his way by harassing other birds that carry between their claws a tasty fish—he flies at them while making a great show of squawking and beating his wings until, in their confusion, they let go the prize, allowing him to swoop and snatch the treat before it disappears under the waves."

❋

The next morning I saw the greenish cap of a small island jutting above the curve of the horizon, and as the day grew brighter, that emerald peak grew larger, the atmosphere around it clearing until my hungry eye perceived a jungled paradise and I began to tremble at the thought of landfall. The ocean was so clear it was hardly necessary to send out soundings as the ship approached a small cove that stretched out languid, sheltering arms. The gentle breeze allowed Shelly and Alexander to easily maneuver past the teeth of coral that glimmered below the tranquil surface.

I had never been in the tropics before, and despite the troubling circumstances I could barely contain my excitement upon gazing into the pale waters at the palette of darting fish, whose myriad colors and forms bloomed and shifted before my eyes. I saw a sea turtle peering up at the approaching ship from deep within a seaweed garden and was shocked when I perceived a look of indifferent recognition in the gaze of that strange creature. Jeremiah joined me to look upon the other world undulating in the waters below. We saw an enormous devil fish that seemed to fly with the gentlest movements of its wings, its elegant form shadowing the sea floor below; tiny forests of waving anemones; and the slow progress of giant *caracoles* oozing along the reef.

Jeremiah spoke in a quiet and steady voice. Yet it was not to me but to himself that he reflected, "I am afraid and uncertain when I think what the future might bring, but there is also a joy that has me awake and atremble."

After the Royal Fortune was anchored in the sheltered bay, Thomas Jones organized a landing party to search the island for a source of fresh water. I waved my botanical manual about, pleading that he should take me on the expedition so that I could look for useful plants to add to my apothecary. I had heard that the plantain was common in these climes, and a poultice of the leaf is effective in treating conditions of the skin, including the sunburn that had all my exposed bits aflame and blistered. He consented and we set off, accompanied by two young sailors who pulled the oars and seemed already familiar with this part of the world. As soon as the skiff hit the shore they jumped onto the sand and ran to clamber up the palm trees that encircled the sandy beach.

They scraped themselves against the striated bark as they raced up the trunks to cut the green fruits that lay nestled at the crown. They hacked with their machetes until they cracked the shells, then poured the nectar down their throats. When they shimmied back down to the beach, the two sailors laughed and rolled about, throwing sand and chasing each other around like pups let out of their kennel, playfully cursing each other's mothers for whores. As we surveyed the landscape for signs of a stream or spring I asked Thomas Jones about the wizened nuts that littered the beach.

"The coconut comes originally from the East Indies," he said, "the fruit of it first brought over by the Portuguese, who reasoned that the similarity of climate would allow it to thrive. I think it was first planted on the coast of Brazil, but now you'll find it on every island and rocky patch that thrusts itself above the waves of the Caribbean Sea. The fruit falls off the tree and is swept away in high tide and storm until it reaches another beach. The nut is not damaged by extended time in the salt water; having reached its destination, it is washed along the sandy expanse and finally puts out roots from the eyes at its top, their tendrils grasping for firm soil until they find their rightful home in the warm sand just past the reach of the highest tide."

He seemed pleased with himself as he reached down to grab a nut and hold it in the palm of its hand, feeling the weight of it and the rough fiber of its skin. He showed me the tentative roots, then tossed the thing onto the highest point on the beach.

I thought I might find in Thomas Jones an ally in my hopes to escape this mad venture. "I wonder, Mr. Jones, how you are finding life amongst these criminals, as I perceive in you an ordered and law-abiding nature."

"Pardon your sensibilities, Surgeon, but I believe I too have grown tired of slaving aboard a merchant ship to make rich a band of speculators."

Without another word he stalked off towards the two frolicking mutineers, yelling for them to pull the boat farther up the beach and take the barrels to be cleaned and filled.

❋

That nameless island had plenty of fresh water. The birds that nested among the rocks gave up their eggs, and the reef sparkled with fish; the pirates decided to use the verdant respite to careen the ship and fit it out as a proper raider. In a great operation the whole crew, myself included to little effect, pulled the ship up from the shallow waters by means of long ropes. Rolling over logs cut from the forest, the Royal Fortune was beached and then held in place with a scaffold built for the occasion. Under the direction of Thomas Jones, the entire vessel was emptied and the cargo stacked on the beach in neat piles, covered with sheets of oilcloth to hold off the rain and damp.

The forecastle of the ship was removed and the deck rebuilt so that it was one simple plane, making a better platform for an assault. The ship was pulled to one side and then the other while the men scraped and cleaned it, removing parasites and bottom growth that had accumulated. I followed Shelly as he went about inspecting the hull for worms, poring over it and pulling them out when he found them. He showed one of them to me, a string of flesh as long as his hand with a toothy mouth at one end.

"You know, the tale of Robinson Crusoe, told to great acclaim by that charlatan Defoe, would never have happened without the boring tongue of this ugly creature." He crushed it in his hand and threw it to the ground. "It was shipworm that sank Dampier's ships, the whole fleet of them returning to England filled with stolen treasures after years of raiding Spanish colonies on behalf of the Crown. A lowly seaman knew the fleet was taken with shipworm; he begged them to repair it prior to the crossing, but Dampier refused, greedy to return to London with his treasures. The sailor insisted they leave him upon an island prior to their crossing, and good thing, for those worms had so consumed the fleet that it broke apart midway, sending all the treasure and the men to the bottom of the ocean, the only survivor being that astute seaman who preferred the company of goats to ending his days with a drowning. The shipworm is an example that small things can combine to great effect, Surgeon."

All of the riggings were also repaired. The blocks were checked for smooth function and the frayed ends of the ropes cut back and rewoven as necessary. Tharinda undertook to mend all of the canvas sails, laying them out one by one on the great stretch of the beach, rubbing tallow on the thick thread as he stitched.

"Tharinda, you rogue, would you be my wife?" said one of the pirates to him, teasingly, holding out an old pair of breeches that needed mending. He was a young Irishman, his fair skin burnt to a deep red in the harsh sun of the tropics.

"No, sir," said Tharinda, "better that I would take your grandmother for my whore, and put her out in the alleyway to earn my evening drink."

Then they went at it until Tharinda pulled a blade he kept close to him and cut the tip of the Irishman's finger clean off. Tharinda held it in his hand so that the Irishman could see the shine of his own fingernail, then tossed it into the waves. I could see the fish swarming to that bloody bit, delighted at the treat.

The wounded man demanded compensation once he had recovered from his pain and the shock of losing his appendage, and Tharinda did not refuse it. After much discussion and complaint, the Irish pirate waving the stump of his finger to make his point, they agreed that when he was married, Tharinda would make the clothes for the pirate and his bride.

✳

One day Jeremiah returned from exploring the island and shouted that he had found some nesting sea turtles, prompting a great rush and holler. The flesh of the sea turtle was dearly coveted by those pirates. That very night, the unfortunate beasts were roasted in their shells with a great popping, and the smell of seared meat wafted over the beach as the pirates swayed to the roar of the fire's flames. Shelly strutted before the fire, regaling the men with fanciful tales of the extravagant riches that awaited them.

As I looked at the group of them they seemed hardly so rough, just a bunch of boys looking to act out a game, until they grew wobbly and loud with drink, reeling about and jumping the sparking fire. Finally their racket reached a fevered pitch and they began to shoot their pistols in the night, and I could feel the wind of bullets in the air.

I noticed Jeremiah stepping, wobbly, outside the circle of the fire, and I went to check on him. I found him on his knees, a brutal concoction of turtle meat and rum bubbling past his lips. He looked up at me, bleary-eyed and ecstatic.

"I am truly here, am I not, Surgeon?" he said, his pupils reeling in the sockets of his eyes. "No more the poorhouse, and no more the lash."

When he had finished emptying his belly I took him to a soft copse of sea grape and let him nestle his head there, scavenging among the drunken crowd to find a scrap of fabric to wrap around his shoulders as he slept beneath the keening stars.

Enough, enough, you say, I can see it squarely in your eyes: what of the business at hand, what will you put in your report? Here am I, my feet deep in the muck and slime of this cell, seated on a pile of straw that scratches at me, talking and talking while you scribble at your notepad and peer at me through the iron bars with glassy eyes. It is difficult to convey experience, the true feeling of events, is it not? There is an insuperable abyss between the moment and the telling of the moment, and it is perhaps in the interstices, in the information omitted and in the shadows of the account, that the truth of the matter emerges.

I understand that a report is different from an account, a journal, or a memoir, for a report requires an authoritative representation of the truth, a clearly expounded thesis, building claim upon claim and addressing counterclaims by dismissing or duly incorporating them into its thesis. You want names. I am at times unsure of my own name, unsure the time of day, unsure, finally, of my purpose, so adrift am I in the ocean of my memory.

Why this obsession with the naming of things? Placing them in relation to each other, sketching tenuous links between them. I suppose that naming the world is an instinct fundamental to society, an act that extends human dominion over nature, for surely, things do not name themselves. They named the ship the Revenge after her decks were made clear. They fashioned grappling hooks so they could seize and hold their targets. Tharinda stitched a black flag embroidered with a dancing skeleton holding a dart, meant to strike fear in the hearts of any who laid eyes on it.

In our time on the island, Alexander and I developed the habit of taking a walk in the pre-dawn hours when the sweet comfort of sleep eluded us both. In myself this untimely wakefulness was due to a nervous condition; for Alexander, his long custom of sleeping aboard ship made it so the stasis of land disturbed him. We were close in age, although from the looks of us he was the elder: his weather-beaten face spoke of years spent suffering the elements like a beast of the field. I also treated him as my elder and thought us both forced men, since neither of us was incorporated into the covenant that bound the pirate enterprise.

"I am growing fearful of my involvement in this organized defiance and intend to bolt from this company as soon as the opportunity arises," I announced one morning as we walked in the semidarkness. Around us all was silent except for the rustling of nocturnal creatures looking to return to their daytime beds before the breaking of the dawn.

"But why, dear Surgeon?" asked Alexander with a wry look. "This adventure has barely started. Did you not sign on to earn your keep and hone your skills in the cutting arts?"

"Why, yes," I stuttered, taken aback. I had figured Alexander an ally, being another forced man in the enterprise, and again I was disappointed. "I signed on as surgeon to a merchant ship bound for trade, not to participate in a conspiracy."

"They are the same seamen you were tending to before, Surgeon," Alexander responded with equanimity.

"Certainly, but their purpose is not the same; they have embarked on an altogether different path."

As we walked along a snaking jungle trail, the first lights of dawn beamed above the single jagged peak that rose at the center of the little island, while around us the air filled with the sound of droplets and a translucent shimmer. Looking about, we saw tiny frogs no larger than a lady's thumbnail and of the most delicate hue, dropping from the boughs of the trees above like raindrops hitting the jungle floor, then scattering to seek a cool and shady spot to pass their day.

"These frogs perform this ritual every single day and return in the evening to the canopy, where in the cool night air they gorge themselves on insects and drink the morning dew, all this in endless cycle, for eternity," said Alexander. "When I was a common tar I was once in the Philippines, where I was sent into the interior of one of those vast islands to secure a harvest of vanilla, a delicate spice that juts its scented strand from a variety of orchid like a tongue, emitting a sweet and unforgettable scent. The forest people there are called Ilongot, an ancient race sheltered from outside influence by the rough terrain where they make their home. My guide explained to me that in his native tongue the orchids that drape their delicate flowers from the crooks of trees are called after the parts of the body they are said to resemble. He pointed to them as we walked—ear, crook of the arm, lips, hollow of the back, cheek."

As we continued our morning walk I was forlorn and quiet as I considered that I did not have an ally in my hope to escape from that criminal enterprise.

❋

When finally the Revenge was made ready, a good six weeks after arriving at that remote island, the crew decided to see what luck would grant them and headed north along a meandering path to go a-pirating. The ship flew under a Dutch flag, fashioned by Tharinda from memory.

The first ship seized was a sloop of little account, took by subterfuge with barely a whimper. The pirates spied it in the waters around Dominica; even from a distance it could be seen that the ship was poorly appointed. It struggled in its passage, despite the light morning wind, its greasy and tattered sails fluttering as it cruised. The Revenge made a signal of distress and a sailor on the other ship waved them in with his cap in hand.

It was quick work after the pirates pulled alongside their prize. They took out the long knives and pistols they had hidden and threw hooks over the balustrade of the enemy ship. The lot of them swarmed over it as best they could, leaving Jeremiah to manage the sails and Thomas Jones at the helm.

The conquest was a small trading vessel, her captain a lapsed navy man who missed a few swollen fingers from his left hand. Although it was early morning when he came up from the hold to apprise the source of the commotion, his eyes were already bleary with drink and his beard was knotted and unkempt. The mate wore a ragged shirt, but the rest of the crew worked bare-chested, their breeches of the roughest sack-cloth bundled up and tied with rope about their waists. Once the pirates had secured and bound the crew and captain, Eaves led a party into the hold and found twenty rolls of tobacco of the poorest grade and a few large sacks of pimientos. The dearth of bounty was distressing for Eaves, who was so determined to have his prize that he organized to take the tobacco—that at least could be smoked—and the pimientos as well, which had no value to anyone.

Shelly had the crewmen from the prize ship lined up and questioned them as to their captain's treatment of them, while the captain sat dull and silent at the end of the line awaiting his fate. Shelly moved down the line of sailors, each more forlorn than the next, but none of them spoke ill of their captain. They said that although he was the commander of the vessel, his love for drink often rendered him incapacitated, but he mostly left them to their own devices and was not unkind in his treatment. One of the sailors offered to volunteer with the pirates: a ready seeming fellow, although his face did not speak of any great intelligence. Shelly was not pleased but could not refuse.

Then a shout came up from the hold of the ship; it was Eaves who had gone back to search each cranny, determined that his first prize would reward him with more than poorly cured tobacco and cooking spices. Eaves came up from the darkness of the hold with three Africans, two men and one boy, the shackles at their ankles dragging on the wooden deck as they squinted and blinked in the light. There was no portent about them, no rattling bones or gusts of history pushing at their shoulders. They leaned against each other where they stood on the deck, but they did not seem to know each other well.

"Look at this here," said Eaves triumphantly. "I found some blackfellas they was hiding in the hold." Eaves pulled at the lead chain that he held.

When Shelly got to the captain he beat him about the face and shoulders with his open hand until the captain begged for mercy with a most plaintive appeal.

GENTLEMEN OF FORTUNE;
OR, A GOLDEN TREACLE
As told to the washerwoman of Marshalsea

It doesn't seem proper that you should have to sweep these filthy corridors, soiled as they are with the refuse thrown from these cages by the inmates trapped inside them, curled up like rats against the draft. When I was a student at the Surgeon's College, there was a room where animals were kept. The rat keepers lavished carefully hoarded crumbs on the creatures; the dog keeper had a long and whiskered snout and a cloying temperament; there were a succession of ape keepers who invariably became unnerved by those intelligent and duplicitous creatures. The animals were maintained so anatomists could practice their small cuts and autopsies: kept in material comfort until the day their necks were snapped to show the students the last few heart-beats of a living thing.

I judge you were once a washerwoman by the strength of your shoulders and the thickness of your middle, and then perhaps you were pushed out from the riverside, your age having gotten the better of you. I wager that being too old and too stout to start in the work of tickling men by the balls you were caught up by the poorhouse, reported by your landlord or another debt holder. Bereft of any children—for, once grown, the children of washerwomen and whores must go their own way in the world, pretending they were born from the ocean's foam or the summer grass. I see your torn and soiled apron, your face red and strained with the force of your exertions, and I wish that I could give you a hand in your efforts; I would put myself next to you on all fours and scrub the flagstone with you, I would lean into it until my elbows cracked. It is a bitter trade—sweeping the prisons to make a meager room and board. I tell you, though, that we are both better off than if we had black skins and were condemned to work in a sugar house on the island of Barbadoes, whose fatal name is spoken in hushed tones.

❈

The pirates of the Revenge took a meager bounty from their first prize: a few sacks of tobacco of middling quality, some dried pimientos to add to the salmagundi prepared in great bubbling pots upon the deck, and three musty slaves who blinked in the light of day. After loading the haul onto their ship the pirates disabled their prize by cutting the mast and fouling the rudder, then tacked away at full speed until the approach of the gathering dusk, when they turned the bowsprit into the breeze and let the sails go slack.

Lighting smoky lanterns against the gathering night, the pirates went into council to determine the dispensation of the slaves they had acquired: Benjamin, of intelligent brow and bearing the grey-whiskered gravity of middle age; Horacio, who spoke three languages and was a master of the mercurial chemistry of sugar; and Jalil, a boy then, whose delicate features softened the gaze of any person looking upon them. The pirates were faced with an unanticipated question: to take those enslaved as a commodity or to invite those Africans—bound by force to labor without reward—to join them as pirates in a lawless existence.

Thomas Jones slyly asked the Africans to describe the conditions of their enslavement, so the pirates could know the consequence of their decision, should they choose to keep the enslaved as merchandise, and it was Horacio who spoke.

"Have you ever seen the inside of the *ingenio*, where the juice of sugar cane is rendered to bricks of sugar? It is a perpetual din and hurry those months after the cane has grown tall in the field. First the harvest, blunt chopping at pulpy stalks in the humid air; then the grinding, the relentless jaw of the mill that consumes fingers and arms. The juices are put to boil in copper pans licked with flames, the reduced liquid transferred and then reduced further, the boil of the syrup melting skin with the splash of its droplets. The workers, naked against the unbearable heat, dance to avoid the ardent touch of flame and metal, the air itself being so hot it burns the mucus of your nose and sizzles the spit off your tongue."

"They say that blackfellas make as good a pirate as any. As slaves they is compelled just like any sailor, a sailor's master being called captain. I say make them the offer like any other man we take." As Samuel Parsons spoke to the assembled men they nodded their heads.

Tharinda did not agree to the terms that Parsons proposed, arguing: "We did not take them and put these irons on them; we did not rob them their liberty. It was someone else who done it, and they allowed it, the proof being the chains they have around their necks. As long as the captain of this ship and his mate beat us and we took it, it was us agreeing to that arrangement, until we changed the terms. We were rendered these men in their state of commodity, and that gives us the right to keep them such."

When Shelly took his turn to speak, he thundered: "We may be villains, but we are empowered to choose the terms of our villainy. To reduce a person to the status of commodity is most pernicious, and who would we be, having delivered ourselves from the yoke of tyranny to enter into free association and mutual work, if we were to deny the same freedom to another?"

The Africans followed the discussion with rapt interest, interjecting when they could, contributing to the hurrah that rang out when statements were made in support of their liberty and moaning with great affect when there was a pronouncement against their emancipation. Jalil took in the proceedings in utter stillness, his catlike eyes awake and watchful.

At the end of the council the pirates offered the Africans a simple choice: to agree to the terms of the covenant and fix their mark upon it or to continue their existence as property. To a man, the Africans chose piracy, and Shelly struck their chains himself, taking a hammer and a hardened chisel from his tool kit to bend and break the links. When he loosed their chains he made to shake their hands to welcome them but instead reached and held them in a quick embrace.

The occasion was solemnized by an impromptu ritual. The pirates lined up along the deck in bright and colorful garb they fashioned out of fabrics looted from the hold of the Revenge. The Africans lined up opposite them and they proceeded down the line, shaking hands and slapping shoulders.

Alexander gestured toward the notebook I always carried, where I made my quick and shaky sketches and wrote my notes in a crabbed hand.

"A nobler spectacle you could not hope to see. Write that down in your book, Surgeon, and render a sketch to fix this moment for the ages."

After the conclusion of their solemn occasion, the pirates took up a whistling and foot-stomping dance, opening several casks to make their rude punch, which was no more than a flagrant mixture of whatever alcohol was handy. There was a grand festival of merrymaking upon the deck to cement the new bonds that had been formed. Horacio fashioned an instrument which he called *banjar*, a woven strand of horsehair strung across a gourd with a broom handle attached to it, and it was not until the rosy hands of dawn crept across the sky that its plaintive twang was stilled.

❋

They say there is alchemy in the process of rendering sugar, a philosopher's stone that transmutes suffering into a golden treacle. The Musulman call it *shakkara*; they take heaping spoonfuls of it in their coffee, making that bitter infusion sweet on the tongue, and they use it in their most precious medicinal formulations. I learned the use of it in various concoctions: powders for diseases of the eye, lotions and poultices that heal troubling lesions of the skin, and a cleansing smoke for the aggrieved lung. Dissolved in fluid in moderate quantity, it serves to clean the blood.

The cloying syrup is decanted to make a pudding; it is blended in juleps and rose waters. Its by-product molasses has a viscous drip, while the white and granular cake is bought by the pound and used up by the spoonful, the crystalline corners of it scraped and crushed, stirred into steeped tea to complement the flavor of bergamot. The elemental sweetness of it is as strong as if it had boiled up through the rocks: it is the dewy breath of roses, the drop from the drooping petals of a honeysuckle, the distilled essence of glacial waters glistening in a mountain pool. Its production is wedded to a steady supply of forced labor, but there is no obvious trace of sweat or dung on the white sugar cakes that are pressed into bricks, stacked, and shipped to all the ports of the world. The blood has been boiled out of them, along with the spittle and the insect wings, the bits of fingernails, and the cane toads that fall into the vat of mixing.

❋

Though you feign disinterest, I see the twitch of your ears as I ramble, so in an attempt to keep you I will tell you how I once met a pirate of great renown, whose infamy was such that his name is still spoken in hushed whispers in the shadowy corners of portside taverns and even the stony corridors of Marshalsea.

After taking the Africans and making them pirates, the Revenge ranged the Caribbean for a month or so, keeping out of the most travelled sea-lanes to avoid any chance encounters with English or Spanish patrols. The pirates did not seem to mind drifting aimlessly until they came upon a prize that seemed an easy take: a small sloop with a crew of not more than a few sailors, say, and tattered sails. They were not so much looking to fight as to build up a steady accumulation of treasure, and every ship they took had some coin upon it, a barrel of rum if they were lucky, some provisions, and usually a sailor or two who elected to join the pirate band. The crew of the Revenge kept growing until Thomas Jones displaced me from my tiny private quarters in a reorganization of the hold. I was forced to hang a hammock in the commons with the other men, and my dreams still echo with the cacophony of farts and labored snoring that shook the hold every night.

The Revenge was travelling handily, tacking against a wind that blew straight on from the west, when a great frigate was spotted. The frigate bristled with cannon but none of the pirates gave it any mind, as they still flew the Dutch flag, pretending they were an innocent merchant ship.

Alexander remarked that the frigate rode high upon the water—unusual, since such a ship was built for transport and it offended her economy to sail unladen with goods. As she drew closer, however, the frigate changed her course to bear down on the Revenge, all of a sudden as cantankerous as a rhinoceros in full gallop.

Shelly shouted to the men on the deck that they should turn the ship and make to run.

"Those gunholes surely have cannon behind them," he said to the pirates as he urged them on. "There's nothing noble about being beat, let's rather show them our tail and live another day."

The Revenge strained until finally the whole deck was leaned dangerously leeward and the cargo tumbled through the hold. In her flight the ship threatened to roll over into the menace of the sea, but there was no chance to outstrip the pursuer, for the Revenge was overladen with cargo and of inferior design, and the great frigate bore down like a coffin smashing through the waves, being handled by able and unrelenting seamen.

The commander of the frigate put out his flagman to signal that the command of the Revenge should slack her sail and prepare to be boarded. Shelly grew indignant at the thought that they should surrender without bloodshed; shaking in fury he ordered the death's head flag to be raised and had Alexander turn the ship to make her stand. As the great yardarm swept across the deck to shift and catch the wind, the pirates made a great whoop to gird themselves for battle. I thought they drew their weapons with a certain melancholy, for their venture had barely begun, and, by the looks of their opponent, it seemed certain their blood would be upon the waters before the sun dipped to the ocean.

The frigate and the Revenge bore down straight upon each other like two charging bulls until finally, as Shelly prepared the pirates to make a sharp maneuver that would let them deliver a broadside upon their attacker, the frigate slacked its sails and put up its own flag: a grinning skull in a field of bones—promising a fight to the death without quarter given or expected, except, of course, to a fellow pirate. They were too proud to celebrate, but the pirates of the Revenge let out a long sigh—I heard it all at once, a great whistling release.

The flagman on the frigate made the colors flutter to indicate an invitation to parley. In response Shelly waved his arms and jumped while his laughter got lost on the wind. They were at least a hundred strong upon that massive frigate, all of them crowded up on the deck to look down on our little sloop; by appearance they were many years as outlaws upon the open seas. Their faces were burnt so dark from the sun that from afar it was near impossible to tell the Englishman from the African. Decoration and golden jewelry glinted among that horde as if they were stars in the bright of day: glimmering crosses and women's brooches, bits of shell and coral, polished ivory and glass trading beads. In the midst of them stood a tall man, fine-limbed, with a face that even from a distance invited inquiry. He wore a damask waist coat that shone a brilliant crimson against the late afternoon sky.

"It's Bartholomew Roberts," said Eaves, a tremble in his voice.

They met long into the night on the decks of the Revenge, Roberts accompanied by a large contingent of the men who had elected him. (He would have brought the whole crew with him, he said, but the Revenge could not hold them.) They were obviously accomplished in the arts of warfare upon the sea, the lot of them floating light as seedpods upon the air as they jumped from the decks of the Swallow—Roberts's fabled ship—to the Revenge.

The pirates splayed themselves on bundles of rope or stretched out on the deck, making little pillows with their bunched-up clothes like Turkish pashas at a wedding.

Roberts was no wallflower. He shook and shouted through the night, working himself into a great sweat as he regaled the crowd with tales; he called for music and got all the men to sing; he took old Samuel Parsons for a dance upon the deck, swinging him like a maiden. Jeremiah and Jalil were kept busy fetching flagons of drink throughout the night, and when the pirates tired of having their cups filled, they put the barrels at the center of their circle to drink at them like dogs, lapping with their tongues.

I heard the final words from Roberts before he took his leave the next morning: "You will find sore pickings in these waters, for they are infested with navy ships; there remains little opportunity for gentlemen of fortune like ourselves. Having tired of this play, we will have no further truck here, for we make our way to Madagascar, where a pirate can stretch his limbs with a sense of ease."

I heard later that dear Captain Roberts was not as tired of the sport as he claimed. I heard he stopped at the Guinea coast on his way to Madagascar and harried mightily the slave factories there, exacting a harsh toll before he was captured and sent to hang.

The African pirates quickly adapted to the work of sailors, as they were accustomed to all manner of pain and inconvenience in their labors. Jalil and Benjamin had made the Middle Passage from Africa some thirty years apart, so each of them had experienced being stacked like cordage in the hold and had been conditioned to the motions of a ship upon the ocean current in the softness of their organs and the bend of their backs. Benjamin was of middle age, of orderly and intelligent character; having a gift for quantities and numbers, he worked with Thomas Jones in the maintenance of the ship's stores and accounts. Horacio was strong and nimble; he seemed at times to hover above the surface of the vessel as he clambered up the masts, swinging on the ropes and gliding down the edges of the sails. Jalil was taken under Jeremiah's barely feathered wing, and together they formed a conspiracy of youth, speaking between them a language that was all whispers and low tones.

The Revenge found little treasure in the weeks following the meeting with Captain Roberts. Her bounty was a few coastal trading ships, most of them not much bigger than a skiff: their capture was a lazy matter, but the catch was also poor. When a small fishing vessel was taken, her decks grey with the glint of scales, Eaves made to seize the nets, in case the pirates should have to resort to fishing, he said; but then the captain and crew of the prize pleaded with such ferocity that the pirates took pity and left them the tools of their trade. Instead they seized whatever liquor could be found and some copper pots that Samuel Parsons coveted for his galley.

Disappointed with the meager bounty of their raiding, the pirates discussed the risks involved in undertaking a more ambitious venture, finally electing to attempt the seizure of a larger ship.

The Revenge was moored for several days in a tiny bay off a lively trading route near the coast of Porto Rico. While at anchor, the crew slept on the deck to avoid the suffocating heat of the hold and swam in the azure waters as Shelly and Alexander surveyed the horizon for prospective prizes. I saw a sea cow swimming with its calf amongst the mangroves; I remembered reading that the first mariners in these seas thought them mermaids and was surprised, for though they swim with languid elegance, their form is broad and wrinkled and could not be mistaken for a maiden's, even from afar.

One afternoon, Shelly spied a vessel that had all the appearances of wealth: well-kept and newly painted, with sails bright and crisp as fresh laundry upon the line. The pirates scrambled to prepare for confrontation, each of their weapons close at hand. Jeremiah and Jalil played powder monkeys, rushing to pack the muzzles of the battered cannon that poked their snouts out the portholes. The Revenge was paddled to the mouth of the bay, her sails ready to be pulled taut at the signal to engage. Shelly strategized that the element of surprise would give the pirates an advantage against the larger vessel, so they waited for their unsuspecting target to pass the mouth of the bay before raising their sail, moving quickly as the prize struggled along, heavy with the burden of its cargo.

The sailors on the prize ship raised the alarm when they saw the Revenge nose out of its hiding place, Tharinda's death's head flag fluttering on the pole. They dashed to trim their sails in an attempt to evade the pirates' grasp—too late, for the next moment the tumult began with the sound of explosions booming on the waves. The prize ship was hit with a feeble broadside; the cannon aboard the Revenge were small and poorly made, although they thundered to powerful effect, making billows of smoke that increased the aura of menace. I could hear the wild exclamations of Jeremiah and Jalil as they prepared another shot.

Sidling up next to their bewildered prize, the pirates launched a series of granadoes that Alexander handed out from a crate he had at his feet—like a street vendor peddling puddings or potatoes—lighting them with the cigar smoking at his lips. As the pirates tossed them up on the deck of the opposing ship, the accompanying explosions were met with great moans and a spray of splinters. After this onslaught the sails of the fine Spanish ship went slack, her complement of sailors come undone, and the pirates threw out hooks and ladders to swarm upon their supine prey. It was with great hesitation that I followed them, taking my surgeon's kit to the deck of the Lazaro, as the Spanish ship was named, while the boys scrambled about me on the hempen rope ladder: Jalil above, laughing, and Jeremiah below, coaxing me with gentle reproach.

I saw upon the deck a scene of devastation. The granadoes—which Alexander had formulated with infernal zeal by packing gunpowder into the hollow shells of coconuts—had exploded with great force, cutting the flesh of any sailor who stood in the path of their deadly splinter. Jeremiah was frozen at the balustrade, his eyes wide at the frightful sight, while Jalil hopped over lithely and moved through the carnage with an easeful air. A Spanish sailor held his shrapnel-pierced throat with a panicked look in his eye while blood pulsed down his breast. The sailor expired under my trembling hands as I sought to place a compress on the bloody mess, my hands fumbling as I watched the life drain from his eyes.

With all the other sailors corralled upon the deck, Shelly and Thomas Jones interrogated the captain while Horacio translated his replies. They sought to discover where the captain kept his strongbox, for the richly appointed ship spoke of treasure. A small party of the pirates went into the hold to perform a survey upon its goods and it was Eaves who first came bursting up the stairs, cursing and laughing all at once.

"Shit!" he said. "It's all shit!"

The other pirates spilled out from the open door, climbing over each other as an overpowering miasma washed up behind them.

The captain of the Lazaro was a youth, the son of a rich planter whose father had fitted him out with a fine vessel to give him the means of earning his independence, and it appeared the pirates had come upon its maiden voyage. The young captain lived in a region filled with bat caves, where the floors are covered with centuries of their excrement. The *guano* of the bat is highly valued as fertilizer, and the young captain sought to make his profit transporting that precious cargo to the great plains on the other side of the island, selling the excrement to plantations where the long tobacco leaf is grown.

The pirates were not stunned at their bad luck, nor saddened by the loss of precious life and blood that their venture had occasioned upon those poor Spanish sailors; all of them were instead consumed with laughter at the absurdity of the business. As the pirates leaned into each other, half-crippled with mirth, the young Spanish captain slipped their oversight. Seeing an opportunity to relieve his wounded pride, the captain leapt at Shelly, pulling a blade from the cuff of his boot.

It was for a moment as if time stood still, all the pirates frozen with their mouths agape as their jest turned to alarm, the Spanish captain caught in midair as he leapt, dagger drawn and mouthing a thousand curses, until his flight was cut short and he fell to the ground with a gurgle in his throat. The assembled crowd stood in open-mouthed silence when they realized that Jalil, only recently come to freedom, his face as angelic as a child's, stood over the captain, his long lashes fluttering as he looked down at the thing writhing at his feet, clutching its pierced lung. Jalil leaned down and gently placed his hand around the neck of the captain, who looked up at him with a mix of horror and foreknowledge. Jalil's body was still as he made a quick motion with his hand, ending the captain's suffering with a vigorous thrust to the heart. A gasp went up amongst the gathered sailors and pirates as the Spanish captain completed his death rattle, his body lightly shuddering. Jalil stood, his adolescent frame slight upon the deck, wiped the blade upon the captain's vest, polishing it to a glossy sheen, then placed it back in the hidden place upon his person from whence it came.

I can see that you are tired by the slackness of your face; I mean it well when I say that you deserve it, that heaviness in your limbs. I have seen your work; you have used yourself well today. These corridors have never been so spotless, and it is apparent you have applied your other energies here. You have engaged with the humble materials around you.

A darkness descended on me after the raid on the Lazaro, as if I had a second eyelid that shut, rendering my vision cloudy. Seized about my shoulders by a great heaviness I retired to my hammock, thinking I might not leave it again, for the close atmosphere of the bowels of the ship gave me comfort in my despair. Jeremiah and Jalil came to offer bowls of food, but I had no appetite for nourishment, preferring to feel the distribution of emptiness inside me.

"What ails you, Surgeon?" The voice belonged to Tharinda, who was at his berth not far from mine in the labyrinthine hold of the Revenge. As a boy, Tharinda had been seized off the coast of Goa by a Portuguese merchant ship in need of a native guide. A buoyant curiosity had sustained him through a life of roving the trading routes from the factories of Japan to the plantations of the Americas.

"I sore regret setting foot upon this ship," I said, "and wish that I was a country butcher now, or a porter, or some other occupation that did not lead me to such tragedy."

"Tragedy does not restrict itself by occupation, and regret is a poor harbor to shelter one from the blustery storm that is a life lived. What is your grief?"

"I cannot slip the feeling that I trod the wrong path at some point along my way and am caught up in a play in which I have no part. I am undone by a conviction that all is artifice and everyone about me a ghost, or I am myself a ghost, a shade amongst mortals, who cannot truly touch those around him. And I am made more ghostly by the death of that sailor, whose wounds I could not repair, whose eyes I saw shake in his skull before he expired."

"Dear Surgeon, I will share with you one thing, which is taught me by my devotions to my mother." Tharinda gestured to the demoness whose form he worshiped, her black skin inky in the darkness of the hold, her neck ringed with human heads. "All that we see and even this atmosphere through which we move is illusion. I have wandered now a whole lifetime upon all the oceans of the world; I have crossed the turbulent waters at both Capes; I have not laid eyes on my people since I was a boy. It has been a generation since I last spoke a word of my own language. I have come near death myself. There is no purpose here, Surgeon, but that which we make ourselves."

Tharinda made a gesture of respect towards me, then turned back to his private ritual and ablutions, leaving me to my solitary peace.

SHIPMATES; OR, THE
COORDINATES OF DESIRE
As told to a representative of the Jamaican
Slaveholders' Association

What is it, what do you want from me? How can you insist so—ever steaming there, haranguing—your bloodshot eye hounding me through the night as if it was I who sought to overthrow your white edifice, to knock down the columns to your houses, to swamp your verandas in an ocean of blood and entrails? I did not organize the tumult that caused such distress—shaking those grand planters down to their knickers gone grey with the humidity of the air, gone florid and musty in the constant heat. I am a surgeon with no allegiance to men, only to their parts: to the soothing of anxious heart and shattered limb, the suturing of split skin, the removal of splinter and gunshot, the relief of abdominal spasm. I have delivered children from the birth passage, pulling from around their sucking nostrils the cling of the placental sack, but I do not determine the paths of their lives. I did not raise a pirate flag on a waving stalk of sugar cane, but if you insist I will tell you more of the tale.

For many months the Revenge was a wayfarer, lurking in the waters of the Caribbean Sea without destination. The pirates seized what ships they could in their aimless wandering until the cargo began to spill from the hold onto the deck. Thomas Jones and Benjamin were in a constant worry over it. Benjamin made it a project to reorganize the crowded hold where the crates of stolen goods had invaded the sleeping berths and teetered into the bilge water. He mustered the grumbling pirates to move the crates of pewterware and bundles of shoe leather to make an extra handspan of space wherever it could be found. Over those desolate months, bolts of linen were added to the catch, and barrels of fine American tobacco, which greatly pleased the smokers amongst them. From one ship they took sacks of cassava being brought to market as feed for slaves and cooked it up with great vigor, making stews and pounding it to make a flour that was then mixed with water and toasted into a kind of flatbread.

Horacio said he had become accustomed to that root when he was a child upon Hispaniola. He had a love for it, even the musky smell that clung to it in the sack, and he recounted its miraculous properties. It is an odd and hairy tuber that you could mistake in the right light for a cat curled up on the deck. It is called *yucca* by the Spanish and *mandioc* by the Portuguese, but the Carib of the West Indies call it *cassava*. It is of such value as a staple that it is cultivated throughout the vast chain of islands of the Caribbean and up along the endless river of the Amazon to the lush foot-hills of the Andes. The most prized varieties have remarkable properties of preservation; sacks of cassava can be stored for months and carried long distances in the hold of a ship or the nose of a great canoe. Horacio said that to grow it is to build a mound of dirt and simply place in the mound a cut stalk that then propagates itself as reliably as a weed.

The durability of the cassava root is attributed to a deadly poison that it carries in its stringy flesh, which must be extracted through a careful process of shredding, soak-ing, and draining the root. Horacio told me that the Carib Indians, who were the original inhabitants of those islands, saved the juice and reduced it to a concentrate by evap-oration, using the resulting poison to stun schools of fish. Horacio used a precious barrel of sweet water and a bolt of linen from the hold to fashion great sacks of the pounded root that were hung to drain, writhing on the mast like grotesque pupae twisting in the air.

It caused a great row when Shelly discovered that Horacio had used fresh water to prepare the cassava, as Shelly fretted over maintaining adequate provisions onboard. He frequently admonished the crew by telling tales of a ship where half the men went raving mad with thirst when they lost their stores to a storm midway in the crossing of the Atlantic. But Shelly did not complain when he ate the stew of cassava and fish that was bubbled up on the deck that evening.

The pirates seized rum by the barrelful. It got so that when they vaulted up on the oily deck of some forlorn vessel they would go straight for it like terriers down a rat hole, barely bothering to bind the sailors before they raced in and out of the hold, carrying the barrels on their shoulders. The rum was mixed into a punch that was shaken up and served upon the deck every night, a lethal brew that provoked terrible drunkenness, occasionally resulting in a nighttime scuffle. Shelly and Thomas Jones were of a sober bent and took to admonishing the men with a refrain that was like a wagging finger.

"Now, now, boys," they would say. "You must not take too much to drink; we would ban it if it could be done. Start up with the gambling and the quarrelling, or fail to keep your arms at the ready, and it is marooning you will have, and that is a hangover that may not warrant the drunk."

To show that they were serious, they once stranded one of the pirates on a beach. He was a Basque with a strong affinity for his cups who had jumped to join the pirates after they took the Spanish sloop where he was a common tar. He had even helped the pirates raid the hold of his own ship, hauling full barrels of salt cod on his back (his captain cursed him as he did it, and the Basque replied with guttural insults spat in his native tongue). Although a common tar, he was uncommon in his manner: when he was sober he was quiet and unusually circumspect, but when drunken a foul temper reeked from him. He once took a swing at Jeremiah, who had offended him by walking too close when he was not in the mood for it; he hit him upside the head and then was nearly killed, as it was but a flash before Jalil had a blade at his throat.

It was this Basque who was punished, rowed to shore, and pushed onto the beach with nothing but a knife and some rope. The pirates circled back the next day, however, and offered him the chance to join them again if he would renounce his drunkenness, a compromise to which he agreed. He even shook hands with Jalil, who did not speak during the exchange but only gazed at the Basque with a curious expression: forgiving, yet with a glint in the eyes

that said he was more than ready to end the Basque's days
should it come to that.

❋

During those months of aimless wandering it was in the
air like a syrup, like the scent of lavender; it was whispered
between them closely, their heads near touching, hover-
ing like hummingbirds sipping the nectar from a flower.
Madagascar. After the men realized that the fertile field of
the West Indies was salted with navy ships, Madagascar
beckoned like a betrothed on a distant shore with longing
arms extended.

❋

You haunt me so that you can collect your fee with record of
my testimony of that little rebellion that shook your island
like a fit of ague. My tongue would be looser if you shared
a portion of your treasure, plying the guards here with coin
so they might let me out to take a little air. I could hardly
escape. There is not enough strength in these sinewy arms
to clamber over a molehill, let alone leap slick stone walls
and embankments to make for open spaces. The teeth in
my head are so loose that the rattling is like a cowbell; their
clanging would undo me. No, it is not for escape but simply
to taste the air, to feel the wet of it in my nostrils, to put
my tongue out in it. Too long have I been forgotten here to

languish like an insect clinging with fibrous limbs to a slim
and tenuous stalk.

✳

In the subtropics there are days when the air thickens to
a gruel, torpid and sluggish. Each moment is like walking
into a hollow of spider web, its clinging strands sticking on
every part. On a ship at night there is an encompassing
sort of quiet after the shouting of the sailors has stilled,
an absence of the sounds that permeate nights on land:
the sawing of crickets in the grass, the throat singing of
frogs, the whisper of trees. On the ocean there is only the
constant slap of waves and the occasional cry of a lone gull.
On those stifling nights when the heat did not permit sleep,
the pirates gathered on deck to share tales and company
in what errant breezes there were. It was as I listened to
the low murmur of Alexander and Samuel Parsons weaving
tales of Henry Evarie that I came to understand the dream
of Madagascar.

"Evarie was a Scotsman, orphaned as a child by the
plague of gin and poverty to raise himself alongside the
pigs that roamed the slums of Glastonbury," Alexander
began.

"No," said Sam, "he was nothing of the sort, but a
London lad, raised on cobblestones and cast-offs, who

heard the call of the deep salt sea."

"Wherever he was born, he was come up rebellious and not one for following orders."

"Aye, that much is true, for it all began when his ship was holed up in the Bay of Biscayne."

"No, I think not; it was outside the port of Marseille."

"Well, either way, he conspired against his captain, for their ship was too long at port. The sailors were unpaid and denied shore leave for many months when they could see the glint of the city across the waters."

"They pulled out on a moonless night when the captain was ashore."

"Aye, and Evarie conspired for an empty vessel to be placed at the mouth of the port and set afire as they departed."

"He was but a fresh-faced boy with ambitions, barely scarred by life."

"No, it cannot be, a man of his stature—he was already a seasoned hand who knew the ways of the world and bore the marks to prove it."

"Perhaps, but either way he soon made a name for himself, for it was treasure that he desired, and adventure, and he was quick to have them."

"The first prize was an English merchant ship returning from the East Indies, brimming with jewels and gold."

"He took the scent of that ship and figured there were more riches to be had in that part of the world."

"Yep, he rounded Cape Horn flying the British flag like it was nothing and took to raiding up and down the African coast, taking advantage of the trade of Zanzibar and Dar es Salaam."

"And it was there that he heard of the great hoard of the Grand Mogul Aurangzeb that he took with him every year when he made his pilgrimage to Mecca."

"Evarie and his fleet lay in wait outside the mouth of the Red Sea."

"And they took the main ship and laid waste to it. Evarie had a Musulman curse put on him for the rapine and raiding that he made."

"I cannot quarrel with you on the specifics—I suppose no man is perfect despite the aura that history grants him—but I do not believe Evarie would have permitted his crew to violate those princesses."

"You may be right, but don't forget that the heat of battle and bloodshed can inflame the senses and cloud judgment. Either way, Evarie and his pirates took a hoard of riches and made their way to Madagascar."

"Where pirates had found safe haven for many generations."

"Yes, and there they established themselves a small city."

"Along the coast of Ranter Bay. They established a city and called it Libertalia."

"It is still there."

"That is what I have heard, and the descendants of the pirates live in harmony with the natives of Madagascar, and no man is deprived of his liberty save if he harms another."

"And they are not lacking in riches."

"Their humble homes are lit up by the jewels of the mogul."

"And the children of them do also have great liberties and run freely, and their dusky-haired maidens sit on the councils where they have a voice in all affairs."

"Does the pirate king Evarie still preside there?" asked Jeremiah.

"No, he grew tired of the ease; that peaceful life in distant climes wore upon him. Grown wistful, he snuck back home and now pulls draught in a country pub."

"It is true," said Alexander. "The pub is called the Spotted Dog and sits on a dusty road. Its proprietor will give you a different name each time you ask him, but he is easy with the credit and has a booming laugh."

❋

Why do you continue to ask me of Jalil? Did he cut the throat of someone important? Was there a warm look in his brown eyes as he passed his blade across their gullet? He had delicate features of an ethereal beauty but was fierce as a wildcat, lithe and quick, always keeping with him a rough blade that was blackened and sharp. A great scar traversed the expanse of his brow and smaller scars were scratched upon his cheeks; Horacio told me that Jalil was fresh from the country of Benin, and that between his people these marks are signs of an exalted status. When I first met him, he made as if he did not speak English, although I always thought that the glint in his eye indicated a deeper understanding.

Jeremiah and Jalil were natural companions, as circumstance had delivered them both to the world at a young age without the comfort of family: Jalil trepanned at the outskirts of his village, tossed into a burlap sack and forced on a long march to be sold into slavery; Jeremiah orphaned and sold by the poorhouse to the shipboard life of splinters and squalls.

Together they explored every aspect of the Revenge; it was not uncommon to observe them looking closely at the tackle and rigging, conversing in their broken language about the system of leverage, pull, and friction; checking their knots with Samuel Parsons, tying and untying, or watching Alexander as he made his calculations. They could often be found in the bowels of the ship examining the joining of the boards and the structure of the keel, marveling at the combination of materials and design that held the vast pressure of the surrounding ocean at bay.

There were many nights when Jalil and Jeremiah stood together on deck peering down into the waves, whistling if they spied a sea creature gliding beneath the ship. The lean of their bodies spoke of the deep affinity between them.

Once I came across them in full expression of their shared affinity while I was searching the bowels of the hold for a crate of silverware, where Benjamin had said I might find a blade to sharpen into a scalpel. Winding through that warren crowded with illicit trade goods, I was stopped short when I caught the outlines of two figures embracing in the shadowy light. Jalil stood, his eyes closed and mouth quivering; Jeremiah was on his knees before him. I saw the silver flash of a muscled thigh and could distinguish a rustling that surged and subsided like waves upon a beach. Even from the darkness where I stopped before turning to retreat from what I figured for a private moment, I could sense the current that moved between them as Jalil curled his fingers at the back of Jeremiah's head and gently thrust, Jeremiah pushing forward with a panting kiss, stopping to take quick breaths as they rocked.

✳

In the West Indies the blast-oven heat of the summer is followed by a rainy season that brings a bluster of hurricanes, presenting sure danger to any vessel caught in their violent and unpredictable swirl. Denied safe haven by the persistent rumor of navy ships in the region, the pirates of the Revenge planned to make for the port of Trinidad in Guiana, where they would pose as a simple merchant vessel and sell off the goods amassed in their petty raids, after which they would proceed across the Atlantic to the golden shores of Madagascar.

It was Benjamin who proposed one last action prior to departing the waters of the West Indies, and the other pirates were swayed by the treasure he described.

"My former master is outfitted like a prince and is rumored to consort with royalty upon his visits to London. He has a plantation, but it is not by the fruits of the field that he makes his fortune; rather, his business is providing credit and assurance to other planters, offering them a hedge in the event of blight or the loss of their shipments to pirates. He handles vast amounts of coin, bullion, and notes of credit. To avoid undue scrutiny of his dealings, he repatriates his profits by way of an annual shipment prior to the onset of the rainy season. He keeps this treasure hidden under guard at his plantation along the northern coast."

"How does he provide security for his riches?" asked Shelly.

"There is only one approach by land, a winding and difficult road where he has armed men posted. On the ocean side he depends on the encircling reefs and rocky cliffs that make it near impossible to land a ship of any size."

"There is no profit if we are broken on the rocks and sunk to the ocean floor to feed the crabs," cautioned Tharinda.

Tharinda was often the first on deck when the pirates seized an idle and defenseless ship. He had learned a trick of eating a type of bark which caused him to foam at the mouth, and in any confrontation he launched himself at the sailors of the afflicted vessel thus foaming, his matted hair jet-black and waving like serpents, so that his mere growl caused the sailors to freeze in terror, not knowing what demon was upon them. He never showed an interest in the spoils, however, preferring to join Alexander in the captain's cabin to look through the logs and nautical maps. He would linger long over portraits and take bundles of letters to examine at his leisure. I often saw him reading them in his hammock, chuckling as he contemplated a particular turn of phrase.

"That coastline is studded with reefs of coral and rocky buttresses, dangerous to any ship unfamiliar with the fatal geography of its shallows," said Benjamin, "but after being taken from the bosom of my family I lived my life upon that plantation. I know that coast better than any man alive. As a boy, when not at my labors, I snuck off to the beach, where I kept hidden a modest skiff in which I ranged the waters seeking fish and octopus for stew. In our approach we will be as though conjured from sea foam. The storeroom will be quickly took, and before the alarm is raised we will be in distant seas."

❋

Under a favorable wind the Revenge made straight for the northern coast of Jamaica, arriving at nightfall after three days' sail. As the dawn spread its luminescent tentacles, Benjamin guided the ship's delicate passage, shouting directions to the pirates who used a long oar to scull through breaks in the reef. Every man went to shore, with the exception of Samuel Parsons and one other, who stayed behind should the raiding party have to beat a quick retreat. I rode in the crowded skiff with my shoulders hunched as Tharinda manned the oars. The morning was quiet but for the squawk of parrots greeting the rising sun from within the dense jungle.

After landing at a sandy strip the pirates moved in utter silence as Benjamin led the way up the cliffside, leaving me alone to fret. The sun was scarcely whole in the sky when the last pirate's shadow disappeared over the ridge. The waves splashed languidly as I walked up and down the shore filled with apprehension. I readied my surgical kit, preparing tourniquets and gathering driftwood to use for splints. I prepared my tools, laying out the needles and scalpels in order, then packed them back up, then unpacked them again. At last I found shelter from the sun in a shaded hollow of the rocks and my heart jumped at each rustling sound nearby until at last I sank exhausted into a stupor.

Once the sun reached its zenith the air began to sound with the crack of gunfire; the echo of distant shouting carried on the breeze. I paced along the beach like an animal trapped in a burning forest until finally I heard the slash of machetes cutting through the brush. Several figures scuttled down the rock face, tossing before them sacks of burlap that spilled silverware, heavy candelabra, and rattling coins as they fell.

First Eaves came crashing down, face stained black with soot and a wild look in his eye. Horacio was quick behind him, then several others, all deeply winded from their sprint through the jungle. Horacio presented a burn upon his hand and Eaves a gash at his brow that caused a nauseating curtain of flesh to hang before his eye, with a flash of skull above it. I led the wounded to a rocky seat, offering a salve to Horacio as I prepared my needle and thread to restore Eaves to a semblance of himself.

"It was spoiled from the start," spat Eaves.

"He could not have known," said Horacio.

"What happened?" I asked, attempting to mask the panic that raced inside me.

"It started strange when Benjamin took us directly through the slave village, where those bonded Africans live under palm-thatch roofs and tend their little gardens when they are not out stooped and sweating in the fields." Eaves talked through his teeth as I sewed his brow. "I thought it odd there was those able-bodied slaves all about when I figured the fields was calling for their labor. They looked scared and broken, the whole lot of them, looming and melancholic. Every one we saw was silent, staring at us with that gloomy gaze. They seemed to know Benjamin. When some of the men approached us, he spoke to them quietly in their dialect and then just turned and told us we was walking right and we did not stop."

Horacio picked up the thread of the tale as Eaves winced and sucked his teeth. "We passed through the village to a clearing where a scaffold had been erected. We saw the grim sign of it from a distance: a great swarm of vultures and carrion eaters that barely stirred at our heavy-footed approach. What was first a confused scene of meat and cruel beaks and the flurry of greasy wings resolved itself in tragedy as we beat the birds away. There were no fewer than eight bodies. Mostly men, with one or two women among them. Their half-eaten corpses hung at unnatural angles, hooked at the jaw with the great point of a cruel skewer protruding through an eye socket or hooked between the ribs with the flesh around the wound inflamed and raw."

"Benjamin startled at the sight," continued Horacio. "I saw tears welling in his eyes as he surveyed the faces of the dead. He called to one of the Africans that had followed us from the village and interrogated him in a low voice. Then he told us that those unfortunates were accused of conspiracy and tortured to serve as example to the rest."

Eaves interrupted. "There was no time for a proper council, but Shelly asked if we were ready to carry on, and to a man we said yes. I suppose our courage was steeled by the sight of that massacre.

"Benjamin led us along a jungle path to the storehouse where the plantation owner's treasures were under guard. We carried the operation off without a hitch. We crept up on the guards and took them by surprise; it took hardly any beating for them to point us to the key that opened the double door of the storehouse, thick and oaken with steel bands to reinforce it. My mouth watered at that door, thinking of the riches hidden behind it. But as we turned the key in the lock it all went rotten."

"He could not have known! He could not have anticipated the consequence of that breach!" Horacio near yelled.

"But it was opening the flood gates," said Eaves, "for hardly had we got the doors apart before there was a great rush that come up behind us out of the denseness of the jungle and every hearty African of the village pushed past to make straight for the armory kept in that storehouse. It was like a delivery of corn in the midst of a famine as us gentlemen filled our sacks with whatever glinted gold and those slaves were just as surely seizing whatever weaponry they could find—hatchets, long knives, pistols, and rifles. They were orderly amidst our frenzy, passing the arms to the crowd that gathered outside, where the women loaded the rifles with powder and shot as the young ones jumped around, swinging the machetes."

"They were enslaved," said Horacio. "Can you fault them?"

"I do not fault them," said Eaves. "I understand their heat, but you know it was from that moment that the affair grew monstrous and bloody."

I had finished the repair of Eaves's brow when we heard the crack of pistol fire from above. Looking up I saw Thomas Jones fall down on one knee, firing into the brush as several more pirates came tumbling down ahead of him. Jones turned to throw his weapon and make his way down the precarious rock face, jumping the last few yards to land on his feet as sure as a cat. He was quickly followed by most of the remaining raiding party, who tossed their armfuls of treasure then raced down to the beach. Alexander was among them, but there was no sign of Shelly or the boys.

Alexander's brow was furrowed and his face slick with his exertions.

"Where are the others?" I asked.

"It was begun in the noblest spirit," he said, ignoring my question, "but quickly spun into something else. The slaves—they sacked the storehouse of all its weapons to prepare them their revenge; they were more than us and had a determination that could not be crossed. Some of them put fire to the sugarhouse, where they had surely passed many a day of misery. The twirling smoke curled into the sky as a signal for the planter's militia that something was amiss."

"What of Shelly and Tharinda? What happened to the boys?" I asked again. "Where is Benjamin?"

"The last I saw of them was in the riot that erupted when the guard descended. I found a path that I thought would bring me back to this cove but instead led me past the manor, where flames were already licking at the curtains. From within could be heard the crash of crystal and the high screech of the plantation master and his wife as their former servants expressed the heat of their feelings that I presume they had previously kept close and private."

The sky blackened with the smoke of many fires as the jumbled sound of horns, screams, and jubilation came to us on the wind. The pirates prepared the skiffs to depart, lashing together two crude rafts to bear the treasure they had seized. While the collective gaze was fixed upon the rocky line of that ridge, hoping for the quick arrival of Shelly and the rest so they could all make their escape, Benjamin appeared, come jogging up the beach from an unknown way. The pirates let loose a roar, menacing him with their weapons. A woman trailed Benjamin by a few paces, a bright scarf wrapped tightly around her head. Holding her hand was a girl child. Benjamin carried a young boy in his arms, whose face was frozen with a quiet panic.

Eaves shouted, "You left us at the storehouse, you devil! If we take you it will be to feed you to the sharks."

Thomas Jones put himself between the crowd of pirates and the little family, motioning for quiet. Benjamin was calm as he stared them down. The woman stood next to him with an expression of determination; where Benjamin had the stoutness of middle age, her frame was slender and her face was lined with a regal beauty.

"We were shipmates," Benjamin said as he took the hand of his companion. "You cannot understand the bond formed between those who share the suffering of the Middle Passage. Both of us were torn from our families as children—the first time that we saw splashing waves and white faces was the day we were sold into slavery. We found ourselves together on that ship, thinking we had stepped into some demonic realm, clinging to life and to each other for what seemed an eternity. Good fortune led us to being sold to the same plantation, where the elemental bond we had formed was allowed to establish itself in a family way.

I could not leave my shipmate here, or the children that we share."

A shot rang out as Benjamin spoke and more figures emerged at the top of the ridge, the smoke of gunpowder around them like mist on a morning lake. The pirates made a great shout when they saw their captain Shelly, and my own heart leapt when I noticed Jeremiah and Jalil at his side.

The boys leapt down to the beach; Shelly turned and laid down fire at an enemy we could not see before he followed. A clutch of the plantation guard surged up to the edge of the ridge and rained shot down upon us as Shelly shouted for the retreat. All of a sudden an explosion sounded as the top of the ridge burst into smoke and shattered stone. Samuel Parsons had fired the cannon from the ship with providential marksmanship while the pirates on the beach made to flee.

It was only once we reached the Revenge that I noticed Tharinda was not with us.

"The Hindu was cut down," said Shelly, choking on his words.

The sun dipped its skirt upon the waters as the Revenge trimmed its sails and made for the open seas.

The Chase; or, a Change of Skin
*As told to a mouse hiding amongst the
hay, his crooked ear marking him*

The compass is a curious instrument: the wavering needle hesitates in its sensing of energetic flows before orienting to its true direction. The cardinal points are fixed upon the face of the compass with avuncular authority, assuring the holder of the instrument that there is somewhere a north, a bearing of southwest, an east that burns at the horizon after the long darkness of night. It is a marvel when it works, the dash of the lubber aligned with the long sweep of the curving keel, the marks on the compass showing the innumerable points between *here* and *there*.

But when it is broken, rolling around on the deck, the post snapped, it is a sad thing. Jeremiah grabbed the broken compass and presented it to Alexander, who held the object in his hands like a dying bird: gingerly, with some disgust. The needle was bent, shattered by a cannon ball that had sprayed splinter as it chewed the deck, when the pirates of the Revenge pulled all the slack out of their sails to try to outstrip the ship that chased them. The splinter took the eye of a young Frenchman who had recently joined the crew of the Revenge—it was I who'd scooped out the bloody jelly and cauterized the wound as he held his other eye shut and gnawed at his lips.

"We still have the stars," said Alexander, "and the well-worn track of the sun. To lose ourselves is not our worry now; it is rather being found."

Before I tell you the story of the fall, let me first tell you about the dizzying climb that preceded the harrying of the Revenge by a contingent of navy ships. In the hours after the raid on the plantation, Benjamin and Thomas Jones went into a frenzy cataloguing the treasures that had been accumulated: counting the coins and paper monies was easy enough, but it was a decided effort to get a sense of which notes of credit and shares of stock could be converted easily to currency. When the extent of what had been acquired became clear, a palpable swoon moved through the crew of the ship, for the amount was sufficient to make each man feel the full expanse of the rest of his days. Over the next few days, while the hard work of keeping the ship oriented towards its true direction continued, a murmur could be heard upon the deck and in the corridors of the hold: a dreaming of riches, comfort, and opportunity that infected almost every person aboard.

Benjamin was busy in his cataloguing and could do little to soothe the frayed nerves of his wife and children, who huddled in the hold, sick with the motion of the vessel. I recalled my own first days upon the Royal Fortune, my body in revolt against the constant motion. The sensation of floating disorients the organs of perception and the natural balance of the body, and beyond that there is the disorientation of being for the first time among the class of men bred for work upon the oceans, with their distinct customs and their language that speaks of salt and the wastes of the sea.

Her name was Antonia. When she first said it, her voice was even and direct, and when she shook my hand I could feel that hers was long, slender, and rough from a lifetime of work. There was a strong affinity between her and Benjamin; they both had about them a serious manner, a certain stillness and equanimity maintained even in the most chaotic circumstance. When they stood next to each other there was a material attraction between them, their bodies leaned each towards the other, almost imperceptibly, subject to a certain gravity. They had a boy of three who alternated between toothy smiles and quiet weeping, and a girl of eight who did not dare to meet the eyes of any person but her parents and Jalil. Jalil hovered by them when they first came on deck. He squatted down at the level of the children to look them in the eyes and played with the boy on the deck; he took the girl by the hand after asking her mother's permission and led her about the ship, showing her its parts and teaching her the names of them, as Jeremiah had done for him.

❋

The pirate who was with Tharinda when he fell had spent his youth ranging the stinking mud flats of the River Mersey until he'd begged and stolen enough to purchase his way onto a ship, where he would at least find a hammock and regular feedings. His hard eyes twisted into a wet grimace as he described the last moment: whipping through the underbrush as bullets whistled past them, Tharinda stumbling and falling as his chest flowered with a reddish stain and his eyes went grey. He said that Tharinda wore a harried look on his face as he died, and I could hardly hold my tears, for I had grown to love the Hindu.

A brief ceremony was held to mourn his passing, assembled during a moment when the sea was calm. Tharinda's body had been left behind among the broad-leafed bushes of Jamaica, where ants could scurry over his deadened eyes and the creatures of the forest push their muzzles at him to see what nourishment they could glean from his soft parts. Tharinda would have wept that his bones did not find their home amongst the flounders—that he would not have the turtles grazing at his eyelashes, mistaking them for a patch of sea-grass.

When Alexander called by playing a slow dirge on the whistle, the pirates gathered to conduct their ritual. Horacio and Eaves retrieved Tharinda's hammock and rummaged through his belongings for objects to wrap in the grayish cowl and launch into the sea in the absence of his body. They gently laid the bronze statue of Tharinda's goddess at the center, her tranquil face encircled by a necklace of bloody skulls, and surrounded it with trifles he had kept in his sea chest: notes and maps; scraps of fabric that had caught his eye; a collection of broken eyeglasses that glinted like the carapaces of scarabs. It pained me to see his sewing kit there, as I would have happily added his needles to my surgical supplies, but I could not bring myself to ask for them. There was a moment of silence and then his comrades started to speak. I could barely see through a veil of tears when I felt a tug at my sleeve.

"I hate to interrupt your grieving, Surgeon, but your presence is required in the hold."

I looked at Jeremiah with disbelief, but as he met my gaze with an expression of acute desperation I nodded and made to follow him. I noted the broadening spread of his shoulders as the pirates began to make their eulogies; I heard Samuel Parson's words as he remembered Tharinda: "I stood guard when he worked near the bubbling pots, for he could not help but slip a tablespoon of spice into the night's mash. He said he loved the taste of it..."

As I followed Jeremiah through the door I had the curious sensation of stepping into a cavernous space, even though the hold was in fact a cramped and narrow warren piled high with merchandise. It was in the little private spaces between those looming stacks that the pirates hung their hammocks. Jeremiah ran ahead through the shadows; the dank space was illuminated only by what little daylight filtered through the vents and twisted boards. I found myself bewildered by the flitting figures I perceived darting at the corner of my eye. He sprinted out of sight in the winding labyrinth, then doubled back to wave me on with an imploring gesture.

Scurrying through the maze of looted treasures exhausted me and I lost sight of Jeremiah again. Following the worried pant of his breath I came to a point deep in the bowels of the ship that I had not seen before, so distant was it from the feeble beams of daylight that penetrated the upper decks; I began to fumble and crash in the darkness, scraping my legs against rough corners until I caught the faint flicker of lantern light ahead. Finally I turned a corner to find Jeremiah crouching with one arm slung around Jalil, who sat moaning and clutching his abdomen.

"He's been like this a day now, and I'm worried he's got something in him."

As I moved closer to perform an exam in the dancing shadows of the oil lamp, Jalil resisted my probes with sharp gestures. I felt the strength of his delicate hands as he pushed against me. Jeremiah whispered a soothing refrain that convinced Jalil to open his arms as he leaned back, rigid in Jeremiah's half-crooked arm, proffering his belly for examination. I rolled up my sleeves to perform a thorough examination of his abdomen, palpating the kidneys and liver and feeling around the intestine to see if there was any sign of inflammation.

"It is like knives from inside." Jalil waved his hand to indicate his abdominal area.

When I went to probe the glands under his armpit, my fingers brushed a growth on his chest that I noted with concern. It was not until I looked at Jalil's panicked face that I realized I was holding the soft mound of a breast.

Stunned, I stepped back. That boy Jalil, that killer whose silence was as deafening as a summer night, became for that moment a girl to me, her belly rippling with the cramping of her womb.

"I believe I have some idea of the condition. I will return quickly. Do not speak of this to anyone."

I instructed Jeremiah to heat some water for tea as I turned to trace the path to my little berth, where I hoped there was something of use among my sparse medical supplies. Passing the stairs leading to the deck, I heard the somber song that the pirates sang for Tharinda as they launched his scant possessions into the sea. When I came to my chest I realized I was not well equipped to provide assistance to a person experiencing the pains of their first menstruation. I gathered some clean bandages to catch the flow of blood, measured a mild sedative to soothe the pain, and collected some dried plantain leaves to make a tea.

I returned to find Jeremiah holding Jalil in a brotherly embrace as he writhed with the cramping of his womanly parts. They nestled together on the bed of blankets, Jalil's skin rich and deep against Jeremiah's cheek. They disengaged with some reluctance as I approached; I uttered bland words of comfort to Jalil and asked Jeremiah to speak with me. We took a few steps away and I explained to him Jalil's infirmity, stressing that it would be imprudent to inform the pirates of Jalil's condition until she herself should so choose. Jeremiah seemed unperturbed with my observations and diagnosis. We walked together over to Jalil and I blanched as I explained that the cramps and blood flow she was experiencing were normal.

"I find myself largely unprepared for the treatment of the female sex," I admitted as I gave her the powders and the rags.

"I lay no claim to the female sex, Surgeon," Jalil clarified, "whatever the particulars of my form. When I was stolen as a child I was old enough to know the special dangers that threatened girls condemned to slavery. I decided then to obscure my sex and, having become accustomed to the advantages of the male part, I believe I will continue to play it."

I promised that I would not share his secret with the crew.

✺

You sit frozen as I speak, your black eyes unwavering as you peer from the hay, your little ear torn in what must have been a narrow escape from a cat looking to make you his evening meal. I did not know then that there was a swirl of history surrounding Jalil, my deadly friend who momentarily appeared to me as a caterpillar that shed its cocoon to unfurl a brilliant wing. Jalil recovered quickly from his menstrual episode—once, when I passed, he grabbed my arm to whisper thanks, the softness of his voice girded by the firmness of his grasp.

After the rushed departure from the northern coast of Jamaica, the Revenge hurried to escape the shadow of that island along a southward trajectory, as if creating distance would still rumors of the bloody conflict that had erupted on the grounds of the plantation. Shelly scanned the horizon with his spyglass from dawn to dusk. On the afternoon of the third day after the Revenge had struck her anchor, Shelly saw three distant ships on the horizon, traveling in formation.

"What's the state of your supplies, Surgeon?" he asked. "I do believe that news of our escapade has traveled, for those ships are far too light for any purpose other than war, and I think there will be blood upon the waters before too long."

Shelly went to confer with Alexander about the route to the port of Trinidad and the prevailing winds. Alexander proposed a change of course after nightfall, when the pirates would strain to keep the ship at full sail in an attempt to shake off their pursuers under cover of darkness. They did not light any lanterns, so as to keep their movements on the deck secret, working with only the light of the stars and sleeping in shifts to keep the ship racing through the night. At the break of dawn Shelly was back on deck, his spyglass now unnecessary. The pursuing ships had anticipated the change of course and were now visible to the naked eye, the target of their furious advance no longer in doubt.

Once the navy ships had caught the pirates' scent, the chase was unrelenting. Each night Alexander waited for the cover of darkness before changing course; every morning started with the sight of those furious harriers pounding the waves ever closer.

The pirates were beset with a grim determination. Shelly hardly slept. At night he worked alongside the men to maintain the trim of the sails and held the line with them during the day while keeping an eye over his shoulder to monitor the steady advance of the navy ships. Not even Alexander would quip when I approached, his attention fixed ahead as if holding his vision to their final destination would speed the advance.

The Revenge continued at full sail, straining to catch every breath of wind, but the relentless progress of those pursuing ships was constant and unceasing until the dark blue of the navy sailors could be seen with the naked eye. Shelly ordered the black flag be raised, promising no quarter asked or granted, so the navy men would know for certain that blood would be spilled if they insisted on confrontation, although the pirates continued their mad dash in hope of unexpected providence.

One of the navy ships, a pinnace as sleek and grey as a shark, broke from its pack, pushing forward until it was close enough to fire a cannon shot that hit the deck of the Revenge, causing minor injury and destruction, but then it fell back to its sister ships. As the navy harriers drew ever closer, Shelly and Thomas Jones conferred violently upon the deck to consider a fateful decision, Shelly yelling and gesticulating, Benjamin between them holding the two back from coming to blows.

"It's not right," thundered Thomas Jones, "to heave the hard-earned fruits of our labors like emptying a chamber pot!"

"We will not have the opportunity to enjoy those fruits if we're torn apart limb from limb, my friend. Let's rather make our escape and seek our fortune another day."

It was decided all in a rush, a quick poll taken between the pirates as each of them worked their station, Benjamin making a mark of "yea" or "nay" beside their name upon the roster, there being no time for a proper council. Each of them whispered a sullen "aye" to the proposal, with the exception of Eaves, who began weeping.

"No, better sink the whole ship and every man aboard!"

Through his angry tears he finally assented, as he loved his life even more than his picture of an easeful future. It was apparent to all that the Revenge was outmanned and outgunned, and the chase was doomed to end with defeat unless some advantage could be gained. At first it was undertaken as a careful operation but quickly devolved into carnival, as each pirate not handling the ship rushed to empty the hold of every piece of cargo secured at risk to life and limb in the course of their short career. Benjamin and Thomas Jones managed the unloading, checking items off their list as they were thrown overboard. Jones was pale and gaunt, Benjamin stoic and unmoving, giving simple instructions to maintain the ship's balance as it was unloaded at full sail.

The operation took some time, a testament to the substantial accumulation the pirates had accomplished. First the commodities were brought up in crates: hogsheads, and burlap bales to be tossed over the side of the ship, and then the valuables—boxed sets of silver cutlery, fine textiles, and candelabra. As the Revenge began to grow a long tail of bobbing goods behind it, there was a marked sense of buoyancy and a noticeable advance in pace, and then the affair devolved into a headlong race to empty the hold of every last item, as if the ship might finally alight to fly with the gulls, making its way to far-off shores beyond the reach of frenzy.

After the first surge of speed that came with the lightening of the load it quickly became apparent that the navy ships continued to make gains in their inexorable pursuit.

It was midday when the southern sky began to darken, and another hour before the first slaps of rain were felt. I could see on the horizon the dark swirl of a great storm that seemed to rush up from the south. Its churn spread across the sky most ominously, but I did not think to worry until

I noticed the desperate scurrying of the pirates upon the deck. When the wind began to whip it stirred and shook the sails and the ship itself began to tremble; it was then that I saw the faces of those men long accustomed to the sea gripped by a species of terror unlike any I had seen before.

Sprites of wind began to scurry across the deck, picking up bundles of rope, insinuating between layers of clothing, whirling up my pants leg and down the collar of my shirt, and the rain began its soggy lashing. Noticing that the pinnace had fallen back and the other navy ships behind had turned and given up their pursuit, I went to consult with Alexander, the wind buffeting me as I fought my way to the helm where he stood with an ashen look on his face.

"Have you made your peace, dear Surgeon?"

I looked confused at Alexander, not grasping the suggestion in his words.

"I suggest you find a corner and make it now, for if you have a maker you'll meet them soon, and if not, you'll know oblivion."

Of the storm itself I recall mostly a howling and a blur that over the course of those interminable days reduced the core of my experience to something exceedingly simple, the edges of my own body under assault from the constant pressure of the wind, my eyes closed tightly against the terror, the insistent whistling and howling winding its way through every crack, the squeaking and keening merging with the revolt of my own body, the cracking of my joints indistinguishable from the creak of wooden boards as the ship was prised apart by an invisible hand.

The steady black of unconsciousness came as a relief on the last night of the storm, and the return to the waking world as an unanticipated revelation. The light changed and shifted with the passage of time as I lay motionless, coming slowly to my senses as sparks of pain raced through my body; I felt a burning that radiated out from my core, and my fleshy form seemed waterlogged and swollen to gargantuan proportion. My eyes were open for some time before my mind was able to distinguish color and form, and then, as my vision adjusted to the shadows, I could perceive about me what remained of the hold: a nightmarish jumble of limbs and boards awash in seawater. It was quiet but for the creaking of the shattered skeleton of the Revenge, reduced to an assemblage of rough boards wrenched, twisted, and shattered by a force contemptuous of the work of human hands.

I became aware of a motionless solidity all around me, the absence of steady sway that indicated there was solid ground below or above. I stumbled out and away from the heap. Beneath my heel I felt the softness of flesh and recoiled. Blinded upon emerging into the light of day, I lost my unsteady footing, tumbling to land face first in the tidal splash. Looking up, I saw a mist rising from the churning surf to soften that desolate scene before fading in the heat of the morning sun.

Although my vision was still clouded and confused, I could distinguish that the wreckage of the Revenge was driven onto a sandbar jutting from a beach where the vegetation was so dense it seemed an unvariegated leafy wall topped by swaying crowns of palm. There was a figure in the distance sitting hunched upon a weathered log, hands clasped on its head. I made my way along the sandbar towards the long half-moon of the sandy beach, limping and scuttling like the blue-gray crabs that crawled over my feet. The waves behind me thundered about the groaning remains of the ship.

As I advanced towards that hunched figure my powers of recognition slowly returned. I sensed by the posture that it was Shelly, doubled over with his head almost in his lap, a most forlorn figure: covered in fresh cuts and abrasions, trailing strands of seaweed, a patch of scalp bloody and exposed. What little clothing he still wore was torn to shreds. He did not stir as I approached, although it gave me courage to see his chest rising and falling with an irregular breath.

I planted myself next to him, falling into a heap, exhausted at the effort of walking in the shifting sand. Shelly stirred as I caught my breath; I saw a look of recognition on his face before it sank again into the nest of his arms.

"Surgeon, were you able to determine who remains with us, the living, and who has joined their ancestors?"

I shook my head and mumbled no, my throat gone tight with the guilt washing over me. Shelly and I both were quiet, lapsing in and out of awareness with the regular slap of the tide upon the beach until Shelly stood, unsteady and wavering.

"Come, Surgeon."

He pulled at my arm, at first gentle but then insistent. I strained to right myself and stand. Arms around each other, we made our way back to the ship and the work of burying the dead and salvaging the living. The tide had begun to rise, and as Shelly and I struggled along the sandy beach we could make out the silhouettes of first one and then another figure tumbling out from the remains of the ship.

We came upon Jeremiah, his body a mass of scratches bleeding an ochre cloud into the creeping tide, his left hand hanging loosely at his side, pulped and mangled as he pulled Jalil out of the wreckage with his other. Jalil's arm was cocked at an unnatural angle, his features battered and purple. As Jeremiah and Jalil made their halting way to the beach, Shelly and I crawled into the wrecked bowels of the Revenge to assist anyone else who still found themselves amongst the living. The tide proceeded to rise and then began to fall again. By the time the sun was ready to make its bed in the jungle canopy, a rough camp was established on the beach, where the surviving members of the ill-fated Revenge had retreated from the failing wreck with the bodies of the dead and any provisions and tools that could be salvaged.

The dead were lined up for burial on the sandy shore. A number of the pirates had been swept away in the storm to make their burial ground at the bottom of the sea, but Samuel Parson's battered body was with us. Next to him the young Irish was laid out. His face was pulped, but he was known for the sash he wore across his chest, and the regal purple of that was as fresh as from the wash. A few other pirates lined up next to them, their lifeless bodies crushed and tumbled by the violence of the storm, and finally Benjamin and his young son, who had been found nestled against each other in the hold, Benjamin's arms around his boy in a vain attempt to hold off the collapse of their world. Benjamin's shipmate Antonia did not speak or cry, but together with her daughter she turned them on their backs and cleaned the faces of both of them as best she could; her mourning was apparent, and her daughter lingered silent and close against their common tragedy.

It was a bloody night as I set to making my repairs with what rough tools remained to me. Jeremiah's hand was crushed beyond repair, the fingers quickly blackening with a gangrene that threatened to take the arm and the rest of him, so I removed it above the wrist—I had recovered my bone saw with my surgical kit, dulled by the seawater but still usable. The operation was brutal, but merciful fortune had it that the boy lost consciousness at his suffering. I removed two fingers from Alexander as well, crushed beyond saving, and at the end of it buried those parts along with the deceased at the high point of the beach where the crabs would not get them. Shelly managed to make a fire, and I was stitching wounds by its flickering light well into the night.

❋

On the morning of the first full day upon the beach, Alexander pointed out the waves crashing in the distance, a sure sign there was a reef just below the surface of the waters; somehow the Revenge had passed through that barrier intact.

"It might not seem it, but it was fortune that guided us, otherwise we'd all be setting up camp with the fishes," he said as he tossed one end of an oilcloth tarpaulin for me to secure at the crooked arm of the tree where I was perched.

None of the water barrels from the hold were saved, and it was not long before all began to feel the parch of thirst clawing at their throats. Thomas Jones and I volunteered to search the surrounding jungle for a source of water, being the least sorely injured, and we took with us as many bladders as we could carry.

We struggled to make our way through the dense bush. Enormous trees towered overhead, trailing vines and flowery liana, and the air was rich with the perfume of new blossoms and the earthy humus of decay. The profusion of plant life served to dampen every sound. There was a quietness in that jungle that hummed louder than every monkey's cry, strange bird's call, or crashing branch in the distance, and we pushed through the envelope of that greening world until we heard the sound of rushing water and turned to make our way towards the providential torrent. At last we spied a clearing in the dense jungle canopy. Muscling through the bush like a pair of wild boar, we came to the edge of a great river flowing somnolent in the mid-afternoon sun.

As we approached I heard a splashing in the river that was neither the sound of rushing water nor the approach of an animal reaching its neck out to drink. Thomas Jones pushed aside the broad leaves of a jungle plant and I could feel the recoil of his surprise. Peering over his shoulder I looked down to see five children, of mixed sex and all seemingly below the age of ten, up to their knees in the shallows, light glinting off their ornaments. They were oblivious to our hidden presence, fully engaged in their play, until I slipped my footing, sending a few small stones tumbling into the river with a clatter. The children looked up, all of us frozen in each other's gaze; the children composed themselves the quickest, silently appraising us for a moment before dashing for the banks and away. A moment later the head of a young man appeared over one of the bushes, and he looked us up and down without haste then turned and disappeared with the others.

Thomas Jones and I looked at one another. We did not know where the Revenge had landed, island or terra firma, but neither of us had considered that the area might be inhabited. We shouted out in English, Thomas Jones in the few words of Spanish he had at his command, assuring that we intended no harm to the children or their guardian, but received no response. We filled the bladders with fresh water, then made our way back to the rough camp. It was Thomas Jones who remarked that the young man who was their guardian was African, as were some of the children, but that others had the deep brown skin and straight black hair of the natives of the Americas. I did not reflect upon it when we first spied them, but I recalled later that I had seen one of those scrambling children with curly locks the color of summer straw.

New Madagascar; or, a Brief Description of a Palenque Consisting of Maroons, Indians, and Pirates
As told to members of the Hakluyt Society

During the time that I spent with the maroons of New Madagascar—which was but one of the names of that enigmatic place—I found my continued pursuit of mastery in the surgical arts sorely tested by the lack of matériel. I wept when my surgical kit was retrieved from the wreck of the Revenge, the sturdy leather satchel with its scalpel, forceps, clamps, and needles glittering within—but I soon found that what the saltwater had not dulled, the humidity of the air quickly reduced to a crumbling rust. Despite my best efforts, my cutting tools had been sharpened to oblivion. By the end of the second dry season, some eighteen months after the wreck of the Revenge, I grew desperate enough to approach Jalil to beg his assistance with procuring new supplies.

When I approached the doorway of his hut I heard the whistle of the wind breathing through the walls, which were fashioned from woven palm branches intertwined through a lattice of long twigs. The thatch roof also rustled with the breeze and the occasional passage of rats and scorpions. The people of New Madagascar would periodically build a great fire upon their hearths, piling on the glowing coals a particular sort of green leaf whose fragrant smoke deters scorpions from nesting in the thatch. Those two-fisted and aggressive insects often lose their footing in their traverse; furious at their misstep, they attack any creature they encounter, and their venom can be fatal if not extracted immediately.

"My medical kit is become grossly depleted." I leaned forward from a cross-legged position on the floor as Jalil reclined on a low cot padded with dried grasses and the crude tapestries produced on handlooms by the peoples of New Madagascar. "While I marvel at the skills exhibited by the native healers in the treatment of all manner of ailments, the repair of gross insults to the flesh continues to require my surgical arts. I have made what use I can of the thorns, sharpened bones, and dried tendrils available for the sewing of wounds, but for amputations and other complicated surgeries I have need of steel implements."

Jalil looked at me evenly. In the play of the afternoon light his deep brown eyes seemed suffused with specks of gold; his face had grown mature and strong since I first met him. The shifting tones of his skin turned clay red, then flashed with yellow and silver as he reached for a cup of tea.

"My bone saws are worn and rusty," I went on, "and the few needles left me are so reduced from use that they resemble the cuttings of fingernails. My stores are even destitute of the simple cotton needed to make proper bandages—"

"Dear Surgeon," Jalil cut me off, his mellifluous voice as always rich with undertone, "I can't promise to secure the things that you ask. The little outings that we take remain a cautious affair, planned on the basis of news gotten from the slaves and Indians in the outerlands, with whom we make a careful barter. But I will hold your list in mind as we plan our next excursion."

As Jalil leaned back on his cot, the dried grass crackling like a meadow in late summer, he flashed a smile that captured the ease and delight of his youthful years. A knocking and rustling at the door was followed by Jeremiah entering the hut with bowed head. Jeremiah and Jalil greeted each other in the language they spoke between them, then

Jeremiah came to sit at my side on the floor, slinging his arm around my shoulder. He was still long-limbed and lean but had matured tall and strong since first I knew him, his hair grown long and its locks plaited into rough braids. He was barely slowed in his physical activities by the loss of his one hand, and both his arms were lean and rippling with hard and sustained work.

"I bring a related matter to you," I continued, "and ask that you consider it is not to chastise but in the spirit of friendship that I report having heard some rumbling as I make my rounds. Your excursions are causing controversy: while you are recognized as a leader among the gangs of youth, able to marshal even weathered pirates with a taste for mayhem, I have heard concern that the raids your people conduct might bring unwanted attention to the those who prefer to tend their crops in peace."

I felt Jeremiah's arm around my back go loose, but Jalil did not flinch at my careful questioning, stretching back in his cot while feigning an indifferent curiosity.

"You know that what we loot and barter serves many purposes, not least the regular supply of those manufactures that resist the ingenuity of the New Madagascan"

"There is no question as to the appeal of manufactures; in fact I am here today to beg your assistance in acquiring some steel that I might make into surgical tools. But some insist that security requires leading a simple life and claim that your band crosses the line more than is required."

"If they would complain, they could bring it to the council to be discussed in plain and open speech. We have our own relation with the old folks, and our activities have got permission from the common voice."

I could feel Jeremiah shifting next to me, and although he stayed silent his grin faded as my conversation with Jalil grew more serious.

"There are none who would question our loyalty, Jalil," interjected Jeremiah, I thought perhaps to cool the ire that had crept into Jalil's inflection.

Jalil moved from his cot down to the floor to address me closely. He carried a scent that had about it a hint of anise and the coolness of a lizard basking in the shade. "Don't make yourself anxious, friend. I hear the worries beneath your words."

As part of their education, the children of New Madagascar are taken down to the oceanside to be shown the uninterrupted horizon above the expanse of the Atlantic, the sand shifting beneath their feet as the sea foam drifts on the breeze. At the edge of the pounding surf the children turn cartwheels while their teachers spin visions of the

teeming streets and cramped houses of London; of grand-
mothers doing the wash at the banks of the Mitombe river
in Guinea; and of the lore of maize, gifted to the people of
the Yucatán to reach its fruitful stalks to the sky.

The battered survivors of the Revenge put up no resistance when seized shortly before dawn on the third day
after our fortuitous wreck, two days after Thomas Jones
and myself had stumbled out of the jungle with our arms
full of water bladders and a report that we had come across
children at play in the current of a splashing river, who
had then disappeared into the brush as if they were never
there. Eaves said we must have come upon some sprites or
else were seeing visions in our delirium, and even as I told
the tale I felt the details blur and slide into uncertainty.
The pirates of the Revenge had been distilled to a small
band—Shelly, the captain of a ship reduced to rubble on
the shore; Alexander, who turned tragedy to farce with a
wry smile; Jeremiah, gone quiet with a newfound resilience;
Jalil, still of a bright and wild nature; Horacio, of boundless
curiosity; Antonia and her daughter, who had no time for
tears; Thomas Jones, the half-Indian itinerant with a gift
for numbers; myself, a failed surgeon and a forced man; and
the seaman Eaves, ever irascible—all of us stunned by the
vagaries of fate. I awoke that third morning to the bluish
white of the brightening sky, my awareness of the crashing
waves muted by the sharp point of a spear in my side.

We were quickly bound, our captors around us chattering in a pidgin that resisted my understanding, peppered with clicks and long, drawn-out vowels. I sat hunched and swaying, with Jeremiah beside me; we leaned in to keep each other from falling over. We could hear the children around us, curious and easy as they talked between themselves; the spear-wielding warriors seemed to be ensuring that they maintained some decorum, and that none of them poked at the prisoners with their long sticks or spoke a mocking word. Rather they stood nearby and gazed at us, solemn and inquisitive.

"How goes it with your hand?" I whispered to Jeremiah.

"They was rough when they seized me, but then noticing my injury they've been careful not to worry it."

I was relieved that I had rewrapped the stump of his hand just the day before.

"Oy, keep it quiet, yez."

The bearer of the voice must have come to English by a roundabout of many idioms, taking his accent from a scouser seaman, although he appeared a small-statured Indian with jet-black hair and deep brown skin.

We were blindfolded and led for many days through bracken and bramble, stumbling, falling in streams, and being pulled along the rocky ground. I recall the surges of terror that washed over me as I was urged along, the disorienting uncertainty at what to expect, the occasional hard reminder of a spear in my side. In recounting the tale of this confusing passage I can also recall the preternatural calm that occasionally seized me behind my blindfold, when I found myself able to give over to the paced stumbling and let my minders mind me on the path, feeling my rattled breath inside me. There is a feeling of swaddling that comes with restriction of the vision, a dream-like sensation.

When we reached the edges of the great swamp wherein lies the settlement of New Madagascar, our blindfolds were removed and the first beams of light hit my eyes like motes, almost grainy in substance. It was some time before I could distinguish the images before me, as all was bathed in the luminescent sparkle of mid-morning on the edge of a vast and steaming swamp, where herons stood like long-limbed sentinels and the reptilian eyes of crocodiles dotted the surface of the murky waters.

✻

It was the pirates that called it *New Madagascar*, after hearing so many tales of the famous pirate haven on the true island of Madagascar, and that is how I will refer to it, but the place had a multitude of names, as the people there spoke many tongues and no one of them owned it more than any other. Horacio told me he heard it called *Palenque de Flores*,

after the drooping orchids that were found in the crooks
of trees throughout the vast swamp. Some elders called it
Cocodrilo Sagrado, in homage to the crocodiles that lurked
in the dark waters there, to flatter their lazy hunger and
keep them from toothsome children. The maroons who
were absconded from slaving on English plantations had
many names for it too; in the market they called it *Freeman*,
for freedmen's land, but they also called it *Starlight* and
Old Man's Swamp; they called it *Whisper of Wings*, for the
place was infested with mosquitoes near the whole year
round, and some of them called it *Sika Dwa*, for the seat
of an ancestral kingdom in the valley of Asante, inland
from the western coast of Africa. There were visitors come
up from Palmares in the country of Brazil, a fabled city
of maroons that had fended off every attempt to roust it
from its lands—they called the place *ki-lom-bo de pantanyo*,
which means "war-camp of the swamps" in their hybrid of
Portuguese and Guinean dialects.

Decisions of any import were made in council meetings
where every vested resident had the opportunity to speak.
Curanderas and *obeah* men were granted a regular position
on the council, to weigh in on matters pertaining to the
intersection of the invisible and visible worlds. Those with
skills in defense of the settlement and procurement of raiding
treasures also had positions, and there were representatives

from each small community that comprised the great mix of peoples found at New Madagascar and from its occupational associations, including the fish farmers, the weavers, and the house-builders.

Council meetings were a drawn-out affair, but the people of New Madagascar are endowed with an easy patience, and each speaker would be pointed and succinct, knowing that the murmur of their statement had to ripple through the assembled crowd from one language to the other until each craning ear had its fill of understanding. The council was held at a plaza on an island near the center of the swamp. When deliberations touched on matters of great importance, there was not enough room on solid land to hold the crowds, so the waters around were filled with rafts. At night each bobbing craft was illuminated by delicate lanterns made from woven palm fronds.

I was there when Jalil was named to advise the council, as he was a fearless leader of many raids to the outerlands (as the wide world beyond New Madagascar was called). It was no secret among the Madagascans that Jalil had been born of the female part of humanity, but it did no damage to his reputation; in fact, it only served to enhance the regard in which he was held. His bravery and ferocity were combined with a powerful mind for strategy and a style of leadership that allowed every person held in his gaze to feel honored. Jalil led a motley crew of youth who aspired to the adventurous life, Africans and Mayans and the *métis* children of pirates who had taken their first steps in the springy loam of New Madagascar, all recognizable by the metal blades they carried strapped at their sides and their flamboyant style of dress. I was at the council with the pirate Eaves the night that Jalil was put forth.

"Mind you," said Eaves, "they do themselves no favors giving him that title. He's got too much a hunger on him."

"Jalil wishes no harm upon New Madagascar."

"It's not him that wishes the harm. This dismal swamp's been impenetrable to date, being it lies too far from any settlement of any size and is littered with dead ends and traps, but time will come when the patience of the *caxlan* will wear thin, and they'll make concerted effort to end the buzzing of this hornet's nest. If I had it in me to counsel, I would say that the people of New Madagascar would be better in the long run were they to keep to themselves."

Eaves' bluster was overheard by someone else in the crowd, a member of Jalil's retinue bedecked in vermilion, and a heated discussion ensued between the two of them. Soon more of the citizens of New Madagascar turned to debate on whether or not their military capabilities should be solely focused on the defense of the settlement or the pursuit of new resources and alliances as well.

I went to sit at one of the children's fires, where attention was more firmly on matters of an immediate nature —the tending of the fire and preparation of long and slender twigs to roast sizzling bits of fish. At the fire there was a young Mayan girl, not more than eight years old, her hair braided with strands of bright fabric in the manner of her people—I marveled when I heard her speak with clear enunciation all the languages of New Madagascar, her tongue flipping easily from the chirps of Itza to the nasal tones of Kru. She spoke English with a northern brogue, learned from a man from *Liverpull*, she said, with that same turn on the third vowel. Dazzled, I lay myself down by the fire to watch the pop and jump of the sparks. All around me the black of night was filled with people, many of them craning to follow the discussion that centered around Eaves and his penchant for the role of devil's advocate.

I lay listening as the girl wove a series of tales in her small voice, half talking to herself, slipping back and forth between the many tongues at her command. Looking up at the starry sky, she made a story for each twinkling point of light, bestowing on each of them a name; she then proceeded to conjure names for the phantom peoples who surrounded the flicker of that far-off fire where a council was assembled to share pan-bread and capybara stew while plotting the course of their destiny.

I watched the sparks of the cooking fire leap and disappear into the black swamp, which echoed with the throaty song of bullfrogs and the chatter and scrape of insects. The child went on with her storytelling throughout the night. Each character in the narrative was granted a history, had words put into her mouth, was ascribed an interest and connecting relationships. I was lulled into dreams at the telling, and as I drifted between sleep and wakefulness I thought I saw shadows flit across the spaces between the stars.

❋

How did you ever hear of me? What was it that inspired you to collect the tale of this ragged little mouse, condemned to purgatory until I am brought for judgment, alone but for the occasional visitor who comes to witness me dredging the canals of my memory where the bones of a ghostly past are sunk. When those relics are excavated and brought into the air of the present, the room grows bright and fragrant with my raving.

I have long admired the efforts of the followers of Hakluyt, dedicated to the recording and publication of accounts of travel to foreign and unknown lands, and wish that I could provide you with all the details standard for your reports, but I fear you will find my memory inadequate. It comes to me in flashes, stray images that streak vivid across the darkness of my fluttering eyelids. The passage of the days is recorded on my skin and in the tremble of my thighs and in the absence of my teeth; swirling my tongue to feel the missing posts, I think my face like a pier, my projection into the vast ocean of the world, the pillars rotting and failing with each advancing year until finally the whole thing will collapse to sink into the passing stream. This prison wears at me. I was not young but not quite old when first put in chains and transferred from brig to brig until I landed here at Marshalsea, and now look at my sucking cheek. I do not think myself given to vanity, but you must excuse me if I cover my face while I talk. I am reduced to rags and near naked in this cell.

✳

While I was at New Madagascar there was one wild-eyed visitor who announced himself as the representative of the last tribes of the Inca. As proof he donned a cape made from the felted wool of vampire bats; it was a regal garment that he fished from a special sack and wore around his shoulders when he presented himself to the council. He was an old man, with a graying beard and stretched ear lobes. He explained that his mother was of a lineage reaching back to Inca royalty and that she had raised him in the rituals of his forefathers, teaching him to honor the contour of the sacred landscape and to burn incense on prescribed days. He said that the descendants of the Inca still dreamed that their last great sovereign waited in darkness for the time of his return, his royal head having been separated from his neck by the invading Spanish and spirited away by his followers to rest deep underground. There, that disembodied potentate slowly grows a new body in preparation of his return. I imagined a human head attached to the body of a jellyfish when I heard this, its translucent ganglia pulsing with the blood of history.

The Inca said that among his people there are whispers of a kingdom called *Gran Paititi*, to the east of their capital at Cusco, beyond the mountains of the Andes. It was established to support the return of the Inca king who waits for centuries in the underworld like a caterpillar straining to become a moth. He said he traveled from his city across the Andes and along the many tributaries of the great Amazon, where he saw no end of amazing sights: peoples who lived in the forest as surely as cats, moving silent and naked through the thorny bush; blind mermaids darting in the waters of the river; monkeys who formed a principality where they grew fruit trees and basked in hammocks in the heat of the day. He crossed dry expanses where nothing could be heard but the twang of long-legged crickets or the far-off crackle of burning brush and followed steep trails across purplish mountain ranges that barely afforded passage to the nimblest of goats. He undertook this great journey to trace the rumor of *Gran Paititi* until he stumbled into the arms of a watchman at the edges of the great swamp. I thought I saw the shadow of disappointment on him when told that there was no king at New Madagascar, and that no one had heard of the Inca.

It is a tradition at New Madagascar that each new arrival is presented to a council where he or she is informed of the privileges and responsibilities of a guest to the territory. The mad Inca was told that he would be provided with a bed in a grassy hut that swayed sweetly next to a watery byway where darting fish were herded into fine nets and fattened. He was told that he would be welcome at any meal that he approached and was instructed to remain within the sacred precinct drawn around the core of New Madagascar.

The Inca was administered an oath, the same that I swore and later violated, promising that he would not attempt to leave the settlement upon pain of death, for the coordinates are held secret and the approach is closely guarded. There are sentries posted all across the landscape, ever vigilant in their hidden outposts, crouched for days in copses of reeds or silent and cross-legged on platforms invisible in the leafy canopy of the dense tropical forest around the edges of the swamp.

✳

You ask the history of New Madagascar? My historian and expert advisor in such matters was Horacio, born in the colony of Santo Domingo in the year 1693 having reached the age of twenty-eight by the time I knew him. Horacio grew up speaking a patois of Castilian and the African dialect of his father; he told me his father was Gola, a farmer's son seized in a war with a neighboring nation and forced into bondage when some slavers came and made an offer to exchange arms for prisoners of war.

Although he was born on the island of Santo Domingo, the cruelty of fate found Horacio separated from his family at a young age to be sold from hand to hand throughout the Caribbean until he had learned all the languages of that region: he spoke French and English with an educated accent, a passable Dutch, and even a few words of Danish, that muddle of a language with a potato-eater's cadence. He also understood most of the pidgins that proliferate in that region of a thousand tongues. In New Madagascar Horacio had ample opportunity to continue his study of human speech. He was quickly learning Itza, which was the dialect spoken by the Maya there. He sat with the Inca visitor and made him teach him the grammar of Quechua. He stayed in the guest house with the visitors from Brazil to master Portuguese, which has the structure of Castilian but is spoken with a sweeter lilt.

He explained to me once that the first inhabitants of the dismal swamp that became the settlement of New Madagascar were Maya Itza survivors of the sacking of Can Ek, the last free kingdom of the Maya that had been established on an island in a lake in the southern Yucatán. Can Ek was sacked by the Spanish, and a few families who escaped as the night was consumed by flames wandered for many months until they came to the edge of a vast swamp. That small group were sorely tried in their attempts to make a living there, having retreated from the desolation of their city in such haste that they barely had enough blankets with them, let alone tools for hunting and cultivating, and for a time they were forced to live on frogs and insects.

When I visited Horacio he would invite me to sit at the back of his dormitory for a chat, offering a drink of tea that he kept in an earthen jar and steeped in the sun. We both slathered ourselves with an ointment against the depredations of mosquitoes, for there was no escaping the fact that New Madagascar was nestled in a swamp. The mosquitoes there seemed at times as big as vultures, circling above the carrion of my own body.

That small group of Maya hid in the great swamp for many years, eking out a spare but peaceable existence along its waterways, growing little crops of yucca and corn in the silt-rich soil, eating the sweet flesh of the freshwater fish that live there, and keeping their children away from the crocodiles by incantation and care. Their quiet refuge was changed forever when the Maya encountered a small contingent of African maroons and mutineers who had stumbled into the recesses of the swamp. The Africans were of the Kru, a people of deep acquaintance with the sea who lived at a great delta on the western coast of Africa. Made shipmates at a slave factory by Whydah, they had cooked up a mutiny when their transport came within sight of the American coast. Contriving to seize the ship, they made a slaughter of the captain and the sailors who had conspired against their liberty, and were forced by storms and the vicissitudes of fate to the same beach where the Revenge was wrecked. From there they made for the backcountry and the stretch of dismal swamp that was to become New Madagascar.

The two peoples, too battered to make war on each other, became blended. The Maya taught the Kru how to catch and prepare crocodile meat, which plants and roots were edible, which medicines could be found in the depths of the swamp, and how to weave the rushes into a simple fish trap. The Africans brought their own lore, having a long tradition of living on the waterways, and carried a determination that knew no bounds.

Horacio explained to me that it was in those early years that the practices of governance and mutual assistance had developed among the Madagascans, only to be further enhanced when they were joined by gnarled pirates flung up from the sea, chasing tales of a place where an outlaw might rest his head, and then further maroons that made their way in from the Spanish haciendas leagues away or even from the wide world beyond, as rumor of that place was whispered in rough alleyways and ship holds throughout the region.

❋

I can say little of the geography surrounding New Madagascar. Rarely in my time there did I have opportunity to venture past the invisible line drawn around the core of the settlement, and in any case I was loathe to venture far on my own, so dangerous and forbidding was the terrain. It is likewise impossible to give a meaningful estimate of the territory of New Madagascar: the impenetrability of the landscape makes it larger than its borders. Without knowing the secret trails that have been wrought there, to travel a league is like traveling twenty on dry land, even in a mountainous region.

In the midst of that great swamp, watered by a fine web of rivers, streams, and underground springs, there is a series of small islands of firm and stable ground—and no end of false islands, where a congealment of tree trunk and the husks of reeds collect to make the appearance of solid ground. Houses are built upon the bits of dry land; temporary settlements and makeshift camps are erected on the floating clumps of river grass that form temporary islands. There are some families and small bands of associated individuals who fashion floating platforms of dried and woven palm leaf and make their homes there, drifting from place to place within the swamp as it suits them.

The architecture is limited by the paucity of building materials, although I would never have imagined the great variety of styles that could be constructed with such a limited palette. Shelly, the former captain of the Revenge, grew mellow during his time in New Madagascar, spending his days sipping palm wine and lending himself as a roustabout carpenter to any who would ask. He tried his hand at building a proper colonial shack from the split boards of a soft-wooded tree —an attempt to recreate the atmosphere of his childhood in the wooded farmland of Pennsylvania— but despite his best efforts the place was quickly reduced to a pile of wood shavings by voracious grubs. Many of the houses are built on stilts, due to the sogginess of the ground, and the thin young trees that make the most excellent stilts are a prized resource harvested with great care at the edges of the swamp.

New Madagascar is not one place but many. The terrain does not allow for large permanent settlements, and the land available for agriculture is limited. The population of the whole collection of tiny villages is perhaps eight thousand souls. Each little village is different, its character determined by the people who live there; some form along ethnic or religious lines. In one corner there is a collection of huts where the copal incense of Maya ritual infuses the air, and in another visitors are greeted by a long slender pole carved with the ritual figures of the Kru. But there was also mixing among the peoples of New Madagascar, which I believe is not uncommon where there is a great crossroads of nations. It seems a natural tendency of the human being to be curious about the other, and such curiosity is only strengthened by the tangles of love, lust, and procreation. The rogue Alexander settled into a group of Maya, where he adopted their lifeways and appearance as much he could.

I visited him there on occasion, for I always found his company stimulating. Alexander had taken up with a young Itza woman who had borne a child by him, and so he was newly occupied with responsibilities, but he would still make time for conversation. He had had himself tattooed in the fashion popular among those people, his arms and chest covered in a jagged geometric pattern that was applied by opening the skin with a needle and then rubbing plant matter into it to give it color. He wore his hair in the manner of the Itza, its reddish strands grown long, shaved at the brow and gathered up in a great tangle above his head. His earlobes were extended as well, filled with disks of polished bone as large as a fist. I asked him if it hurt.

"It's a pinching when you first put holes in the lobes, but then they are stretched over time, an operation that is barely noticed."

He held his baby as he spoke; she wriggled in his burly arms. She had fine features and the black hair of her mother, but her eyes were the same piercing green as her father's.

❋

The economy of New Madagascar was not wholly self-contained. It would be impossible to provide for all the needs of the inhabitants based on the inherent capacities for manufacture and production contained within the swamp, although the population was most ingenious in their exploitation of the landscape. They grew their produce on manufactured floating islands called *chinampas*, created by making long platforms of woven aquatic plants, then dredging muck from the bottom of the swamp to lay a bed of soil upon the woven mat. The swamp was filled with a network of weirs and netted areas where there were raised several varieties of fish and a freshwater crab that was native to those parts, which in molting season is soft shelled and when harvested is ground up into a paste and used in all the cooking. Yucca mounds dotted the spaces between every house as well as every other place that could be put to its production. The long fronds of the plant swaying above that prized root can be found in every corner of the settlement.

Although the Maya everywhere have a reverence for their native maize, the environment of the swamp does not very well suit its cultivation, so the production of maize is largely a ritual affair. Restricted to a few small fields, the planting of maize was accompanied by song and the banging of a drum. The eating of it was largely limited to when they made the dumpling they call *tamale* for their ritual, the insides filled with beans and bits of aromatic herbs and crab paste.

Where possible, they planted banana and plantain trees, and in some parts of the swamp they built walls of stone and mud to create submerged fields of rice. There were stands of sugar cane—I spent several idle afternoons chewing at those sticks, the juice dripping down my whiskered chin. There was a little tobacco grown, its leaves dried in shade-houses to keep off the sun, and the older Itza Maya and the Kru would roll it into cigars and smoke them, as they sat with their veiny legs in the black waters to keep cool during the long sunsets of summer.

The maroons made salt from the ash of a variety of palm tree, and they made butter by clarifying the fat from a grub that made its home in those same trees. There was little game in the swamp, although crocodiles might be harvested for feasts—despite their gruesome appearance, they have a most tender flesh when properly prepared.

The viability of any community is measured by the maintenance of reserves to provide sustenance in lean seasons. The Madagascans keep their stores in little houses placed upon tall swaying poles hidden amid copses of tall trees scattered throughout their territory. Thomas Jones, the former quartermaster on the Revenge, was involved in ensuring that the depots were filled with sacks of yucca flour, rice, and a powdered meal made out of crabs. He had learned the art of smoking meat when he was a child, so the stores soon included bricks of smoked crawfish wrapped in banana leaf. Having formed a sort of brother-hood with Benjamin, Thomas Jones proposed an alliance with Benjamin's widow Antonia after she and her daughter completed their time of mourning, and Antonia received him.

Although the residents of New Madagascar have become adept at wresting produce from that stubborn land, there will always be an absence of manufactures there, for they have no metals, and there is not enough hardwood for them to make any form of machinery. There are few stones to crush the yucca or make millstones for the processing of corn. In the absence of any metallurgy, the place is also short on weaponry, and a sharp-edged machete is highly valued. The cut of a steel blade is indispensable for clearing the fields and the vines from around their houses. In place of shot the maroons will often arm the few muskets that they possess with steel buttons and gravel. The Madagascans have informants and sympathizers amongst the slaves and Indians that live in that sparsely populated and mosquito-ridden corner of the Spanish empire. Through those intermediaries they are able to trade beeswax and honey for machetes, weapons, and textiles, as well as the cooking pots and other necessities that are requested from the council at home.

✻

I once asked Horacio if he had ever heard of maroons when he was a slave and he told me this story: "The first maroon that I ever heard of was an old man who had lived his life a slave, seen his children born under slavery and sold away. He was patient with his suffering until the day came that his wife was took from him. She was gone ill with influenza and died in the field, her last breath passed where she worked at pulling the weeds from around the tobacco plants. She could easily have survived had she been given a few days of bedrest to recover, but her utility to the plantation was long past and the master saw an opportunity to be rid of her by natural means. The old man grew cold and hard after that.

"The first time he ran away, the old man went to live in the forest, making his bed in a simple lean-to that he built between the bushes. The old man did his best to provision himself from the produce of the forest, catching birds with snares that he placed in the tree branches, digging roots, and chewing at the bitter leaves, but he could not survive without pilfering a little. A few of the slaves from the plantation who knew the old man, understanding how the loss of his wife had unhinged him, supplied him with whatever they could spirit out to him where he hid in the depths of the forest.

"When he was caught, the master had him striped with thirty lashes, a heavy burden even for a younger man, but the old man bore it like a rock. He was in the field the day after, his back still breaking bloody when he moved, but he did not complain. The old man waited for his wounds to crust over before he started gathering supplies to take himself deeper into the woods and then off he went again.

"We children had a name for him. We called him Old Moss, as that is how we figured him, having adopted great powers of camouflage that allowed him to hide from the hunting parties the master sent out after him. We figured he could take on the likeness of all the aspects of the forest: the mottled grey of the granite boulder, the thorny bush, the spider moss. When we went to collect firewood we left him little offerings and put a scare on each other by invoking his presence—I imagined him with wild yellow eyes, taking his picnics with the animals of the forest, his dress a cape of parrot feathers, his closest companion a gentle deer—but eventually he was caught again, this time betrayed by another slave who met with him on moonless nights and provided him yucca flour, who was caught returning and tortured until he revealed the details of the arrangement.

"This time the old man was dragged in and hobbled, his left foot removed so that he could not think of going again. But, as I said, the old man was a rock; he preferred his liberty and had decided that the passing of his wife was occasion for the termination of his time of bondage. When he recovered from the outrage committed upon him he fashioned himself a crutch and made again for the forest, beginning first on well-worn paths, then winding through the brush. His absence was discovered the morning after his flight and the master became incensed—I think it was less the impact to his livelihood, for the old man was well past his days of productive work, than that the master could not tolerate the simple act of defiance.

"The master organized a party to hunt and capture the old man, taking the cruelest of his hunting dogs, who could face down the fiercest wild boar and come out from the encounter in one piece, and he gave their handlers orders to set the dogs upon the old man once they found him, to bring him back dead and in pieces. They quickly found him, for despite his stony will he was limited in his locomotion. I do not know if it was that he knew the mark of death had been put upon him, or simply that he would not abide another hour of his life to be spent in captivity, but when the hunting party had him backed up onto a canyon with a swift running stream below and the slavering dogs leapt towards him, he preferred his liberty so much that he threw himself into the stream, where his body was quickly broken on the rocks and swept away.

"We children continued to leave him offerings when we advanced into the forest to collect brush for our dinner fires. We carefully placed them in a ring of stones so he would know that we loved him."

Empire of Dreams; or, the Mechanics of Flight
As told to a judge of the Admiralty Court

Although your countenance and authority make me tremble, it is also a relief to finally contemplate your powdered wig and black frock. There is a certain comfort in the full regalia of the law after the timeless misery of my languish in the stony cells of Marshalsea. While it may only be due to a writ of *habeas corpus* that I have your attention—scratched into the margins of a discarded broadsheet and submitted to the Court through the graces of a sympathetic washerwoman—I would plead you lend me a generous ear while I demonstrate my innocence of the crimes with which I am charged. Should you ask yourself where is the body that has been produced, I humbly direct your attention to this pile of rags and stringy hair that sways before you, rambling.

You will find beneath this shrunken exterior, greatly diminished from an already modest stature, an inmate detained on charges of piracy and rebellion in what now seems a distant era—such is the mystery of time and memory, is it not? Each day that accumulates is a succession of moments that gather themselves into a shadowy mass and fill up the room, looming overhead. For the passage of an eternity this inmate has suffered the cell where the barred window catches the sun for only a few moments in the blinding blur of day, where the air is always damp, where the walls sweat in the brick-oven heat of summer and ice over in the winter. Where the only company is vermin and filth and whatever unfortunate wreck is made my cell-mate, at least until the drone of my tale-telling overwhelms his reason and he begs to be transferred.

It was two years after the wreck of the Revenge when Jalil proposed that the people of New Madagascar construct a fleet of *piraguas* for trading along the Atlantic coast. Many remote villages scraped out an existence there at the edges of the empire, offering a chance for the Madagascans to barter the wild honey they harvested from the buzzing hives found deep in the great swamp, floral with the nectar of delicate blooms flowering at the crooks of mossy trees. Jalil ventured that the little trading fleet could exchange that sweet elixir for machetes, worn knives, and any other scraps of metal that could be turned to shot and arrow points in smoking forges stoked with dried bog and bamboo shavings. Shelly amended the proposal to add the establishment of a small fishing camp at the coast, where a web of streams and small rivers let out their silted discharge into the wide Atlantic. He argued that the catch from the fecund reef could be dried and smoked for ease of transport and packed into sacks of woven grasses to be carried back to the settlement.

When they first heard that Jalil and Shelly had petitioned for the construction of a fleet of ocean-going craft, the old men laughed and pointed at the elegant silhouette of a heron floating through the evening air.

"You would have your boats harnessed to the birds to fly them over the treetops?"

But Jalil and Shelly had planned well, anticipating the obstacles to their ambitions, most of all the reluctance of the maroons of New Madagascar to expose their guarded freedom to the world. Jalil had organized his band of peacock warriors to survey the routes to the sea, tramping through the deep jungle until they discovered a secure passage. By widening one stream at a narrow bend and softening a few sharp curves on another, a small fleet of piraguas could be transported down to the coast. Shelly had identified a lagoon by the coast where the fleet of ships could be assembled and sheltered between their sorties.

Jalil and Shelly engaged in some politicking to persuade the leaders of New Madagascar of their good intentions, bringing cigars to the *obeah* men, strings of special seeds to the *curanderos* and *curanderas*, and explaining to the heads of the various guilds how their scheme would improve the general welfare. The lead opponent to their proposal was a fierce young woman with a dark copper hue to her cheek, the third generation of a family of fish farmers and head of their guild, who stood before the council to oppose any effort to expand the links of trade with the outerlands.

"The fabric of our union is as delicate as one of our nets floating in the dark of these waters, each person one of the strands that together constitute a stronger weave. The Whisper of Wings is still gathering its energies and is not ready for truck with the wider world," she said.

Shelly, ever the realist, invoked the hard threats to New Madagascar in his reply: "Our continued defense requires metal spears and arrow tips to find the joints between Spanish plates of armor. It requires lead shot for the few rusty muskets that we keep at hand. And it requires a well-fed people."

"The Whisper of Wings has grown strong in isolation—it is too dangerous to invite this exchange with the *caxlan*," said the young woman. "We may barter more than we wish without knowing it."

"It is foolish to think that we will be protected forever in this swamp. The Spanish know well we are here, and their assaults grow more coordinated with each attempt."

It was many council meetings held in the hot soup of the night before the question of forging a tentative link with the sea and the wide world beyond was resolved: many nights of robust conversation punctuated by tears of anxiety, pleas to ancestors and forest spirits for guidance, and long, rambling tales weaving in and around the question under consideration. The measured talk of cool heads held the problem like a knot of mahogany, feeling its weight: the pocked surface of it, the promises suggested in the mass of it, the core of dark portents that seemed to lurk beneath the worn and impenetrable surface.

❊

When Jalil was first come aboard the Revenge, since reduced to driftwood and pulp by the action of the pounding surf, he was a slight boy of lean and murderous hand. After washing up on the shores of New Madagascar I watched him grow and take a seat at the head of a band of warriors made up of the multi-hued and polyglot youth that were the generation of New Madagascar—come up free outside the iron links of bondage and peonage. As Jalil matured his biology expressed itself, softening and filling his form. Jalil played his changing shape with grace. There were days when he wore his hair in beaded braids and put a grass skirt around his waist, and he and Jeremiah walked with their bodies intertwined, arms around each other's shoulders. They walked together the same when Jalil wore the hides and feathers of impending war.

Jeremiah was always kind to me. Although relentlessly busy with his duties and responsibilities, he made sure to visit me at the cot I kept in the guesthouse, inquiring whether I had adequate supply of tools and provisions.

"You are well, Surgeon?"

"I am running short of plantain leaves to make poultices. I need a supply of hardwood to make splints, and I need more of that remedy that quiets the cough of my neighbors' children," I would say.

"And you, Surgeon, you are well supplied? You have blankets to hold off the wet chill of these rainy-season nights?"

"I have a blanket, but I must admit the roof here needs some thatching. The rain comes in like water through a sieve when it gets to storming."

The next day, Jeremiah would be at my hut with one of his rough companions, weaving new thatch into the roof, his one able hand working nimbly with the stump of the other.

❋

At first it was barely an idea, as ephemeral as a tuft of dandelion seed floating on an early summer wind.

❋

At the outskirts of the swamp there is a forest of long, straight trees, whose timber is perfect for making the water-craft called *piragua*. Fashioned in the shape of a long cigar with a pitch-blackened hull, the piragua is made by taking the trunk of a tree that has timber both lightweight and resilient. The bark is stripped and the log set on stands to cure in the air; once tempered, the log is hollowed out by the progressive setting of controlled fires, while the hull is shaped by the measured blows of a razor-sharp machete. It is a simple vessel that is remarkably sturdy. When crafted by a master hand, a piragua cuts through the waves as smoothly as a seal.

Shelly invited me to the camp established at the outskirts of the swamp to see the shipyard where the modest fleet of New Madagascar was being built. As we walked towards the camp by a winding and obscure path, Shelly told me he had felt possessed as if by an outside force since he first set his thoughts on feeling the bob of waves beneath him again.

As soon as we arrived at the camp he took to working on the nearest ship with determination, intent on his ambition of returning to the tides.

The shipyard was a clearing in the jungle where perhaps twenty citizens of all ages worked together at shaping the piraguas and bubbling tree sap into a dark and oily pitch. I found Eaves working at a mighty log that was easily eight yards long, a formidable ship that could hold more than a score of determined paddlers. I asked Eaves what was the purpose of such a great ship—it seemed far grander than necessary for simple trading or fishing.

"You ask a reasonable question, as by the looks of it I'd say this long ship is built with more in mind than a little trading in crab paste and honey."

"What do you mean?"

"I mean that six days hard paddling from the coast there is a town at the edge of Panama, where there are weapons and gold and the opportunity to make a reputation." Eaves made his comment with a raised brow, then quickly changed the subject. "I'll tell you one thing, Surgeon: thinking on the pull of the tide sets my thoughts on the soot and the reek of London and turns my heart to pounding. It conjures the stink of Londoners pressed in all together by the narrow streets. I find myself missing the assorted crowd, the yelps of the street vendors and the beggars, the determined faces of parents making their best efforts to keep their children fed and catch what moments of peace can be found. Remember the cry and circle down among the docks, the collection of humanity that pins its hopes and desperation to those cobbled streets? The bustle of the pavements, the cackle of fish-wives and whores as they compare their wares, the turn and clang of the carriage wheels, the long glances, the furtive glances, the sing-song of children spilling in the streets—when those recollections start their steady roll I get quiet and feel a pulling.

"I had a sister nine years younger than me—when I left she was clinging snot-faced to the skirts of my mother. Thinking on her gets me feeling desperate for news from home, for I figure her a woman now and subject to all the viciousness that can bring. Our father was lost to the tides of gin that wash up on a London family's shores now and again. It's thinking of my fatherless sister without the guidance of her brother that puts me to weeping."

Eaves was a hard man whose rough exterior did not suggest regret or sentiment, and I felt a pulling in my gut when I saw his eyes go teary. My own childhood was in the countryside: grey in winter and flowering green in summer, a world of clipped greetings to neighbors while switching the cow along the lane and stolen moments in meadows of spring wildflowers. I'd never known London well enough to grow any great affection for it. I was a student when there, just another beetle scurrying to hide my ball of dung in that cacophony, but as Eaves spoke I recalled moments of walking anonymous in the swirling streets of that city, swaddled in a comforting certainty that I was but one among many between the flickering shadows of the street torches, alone and secure in my powers. Thinking back on those times when I felt a sense of possibility made me wistful for the smoke and the retch of London.

"New Madagascar has been a welcome respite, but I am gripped by a growing curiosity to learn again what the world might have to offer," Eaves muttered at last, turning to his work even as he spoke.

I walked away with a quick farewell but after several paces I realized the shadow of a suggestion in his speech. Glancing back, I saw the former seaman hard at work, no longer paying me any mind.

Every dwelling in New Madagascar maintained a chamber pot where the residents deposited their excrement as well as a separate jar for urine, and along public ways and plazas there were areas screened off by light walls of long rushes behind which the inhabitants could relieve themselves. The urine was sprinkled amongst the fields as crops watered with that effluent were found to thrive. The management of the heavier excretions was a matter of public charge, and the work of handling and removing the stuff was a regular assignment that no able-bodied adult was exempt from, not even the most venerated of the *curanderos*, who would strip down to just one piece of their sacred vestment when assigned the duty of collecting nightsoil.

When first assigned that duty I made most desperate protestations, still clinging like a tick to the imagined privilege of my station; it was Jeremiah who gently explained that I would not have the opportunity to continue my practice of the delicate patching of wounds, bloody amputation, and bone-setting if I should also have to grow crops and tend chickens to feed myself. There being no system of money at New Madagascar to permit the fish farmer and the carpenter to sell to one another the product of their labors, the continued practice of my specialized skills demanded my participation in the common labor of the community, including the dreaded nightsoil detail.

One evening I was fortunate enough to be assigned to work with Alexander. Since he had started a family, his mingling had got less, and I was sorely missing his company. Even when I called on him he was often busy tending to his infant daughter, his young wife, or her wizened mother, a grandmother several times over who was venerated in the family, as elder women of the Maya culture are. The grandmother was understandably cautious of her daughter's choice of a leathery, red-headed seaman for her mate, although encouraged to see him adopt their people's ways. Whenever I encountered Alexander I marveled at his ornament, for his adoption of Maya life-ways was complete. He wore only the light loincloth that was their customary dress.

"Do you not at times get to thinking on the wider world?" I asked of Alexander, my words with Eaves having uncoiled a curiosity that grew and stretched within me.

"The truth is I have finally found myself content with the world as it meets me, figuring if you observe one thing closely enough and with complete attention you can know all there is to know, for in each thing is the seed of every other."

"I had no idea you were becoming a philosopher."

I laughed as we shouldered a great jug full of excrement to move to the waiting barge, the smell of it wafting in a great cloud that dissipated in the coolness of the night air. Alexander looked at me closely as we emptied the vessel into the waiting barge; he squinted his eyes at me and I could feel the flush of my cheeks beneath his inquiring gaze until I was forced to look away for fear he should perceive my secrets.

"You have a right to seek your happiness, Surgeon. You may not find it, but you surely have the right to seek it."

I had so long felt pulled from one disaster to the next

that to hear Alexander speak of a right to seek happiness stunned me into silence—until he started at the joking about our nighttime duties, up to his elbows in shit.

❋

Throughout my time at New Madagascar the Spanish and their mercenaries persisted in their attempts to penetrate the forbidding swamp to raid and harass the maroons. These raids mostly ended in slow attrition, if not outright mayhem, for the Spanish forces, but securing this outcome required bloody effort on the part of the settlement's defenders. While the fleet of piraguas was being built, Jeremiah came for me in the black of night carrying a torch fueled by the derived fat of mealy worms, which curled tongues of black smoke as it sputtered. I started awake, my eyes still fixed on the dreams that had galloped before them only moments before: vivid and distorted recollections of my grim childhood; the strained faces of my father and mother; a cavalcade of clowns sauntering through this tableau of childhood misery accompanied by a herd of the strangest creatures, huge lumbering beasts that had the great shoulders of musk oxen. The beasts strained to pull along the world in its circuit; in place of the wide-eyed blandness of an ox-face they had human faces, which contorted and seized as they moved through likenesses of every human emotion.

Jeremiah's own face was frozen into an anxious mask, his dirty skin bloodied with scratches. As I sat up to make myself awake he threw my clothes and sandals at me; he was not solicitous and did not apologize for interrupting my sleep.

"Where is your kit for stitching?"

I motioned at the little trunk that held my few personal possessions and the tattered remnants I called my surgical kit. Jeremiah grabbed the kit with one hand and put his other arm around me, the stump of his hand at my shoulder, and led me out into the night. I could feel the urgency of his pull, his whole body slick with sweat, his rapid and shallow breath. Jeremiah bundled me into a small boat that lay waiting with another youth in it, whom I recognized as one of Jalil's gang, his eyes glowing in the bed of soot that streaked his face. After Jeremiah fixed the torch at the bow he and the youth began to paddle furiously, cutting through the black water with the smooth and soundless motion of a snake. I thought to speak, to ask what was the emergency, but the look of grim determination on their faces silenced me.

We came to the outskirts of the swamp where a great blaze could be seen, flames licking at the night sky, sparks flying up and crackling away in the field of stars. Approaching the conflagration I could see the silhouettes of many figures flitting before the flames. As the canoe made to land Jalil ran up with a torch in hand, his preternaturally calm face lined with anger and fatigue. He hauled the canoe up to the shore with a heave and grabbed my arm to pull me out of the boat and hustle me along.

"Hurry, they are lucky to have made it this long."

As Jalil tugged at me I felt the enormous strength that was held so casually in those wiry arms; he was dressed in his war clothes and there was the smoke of adornment around his eyes. His hair was made into braids with the fluff of soft feathers quivering in the heat of the flames. He dragged me along until we got up close to the dancing flames, where I first got a sense of the urgency of the matter.

There were five of Jalil's gang being tended around the fire, all of them exhibiting serious wounds: gaping gashes at their breasts; one of them cut severely across the face; another bleeding copiously from his chest, where pellets of shot were lodged underneath his skin, creating a rolling landscape. I settled on the tending of one of the gang who had barely stopped being a boy, his cheeks soft and untouched by the down of adulthood. His arm was nearly severed and the boy would have bled out already were it not for the tourniquet tied securely above the cut; I knew it was Jeremiah that had dressed the terrible wound, for he tied the knots as I had demonstrated him when he was my apprentice. As I placed a strop of leather between the boy's teeth I bade him look away so I might prod the wound to determine if the arm could be saved.

"We were on our regular patrol and came upon a good dozen of them *caxlan*, armed for mayhem, who were sneaking up to attempt to come into Madagascar and make some trouble. We engaged them and finally did get them, but they had fine blades and plenty of shot and they got some of our number in the exchange. It was finally with sharpened sticks that we got them to fall down." Jalil's voice cracked with frustration as he spoke. "Had we better armament none of ours would have been wounded, and we would have ended them when we first saw them, with no loss to us, though we ended them nonetheless." Jalil gestured. I could see laying in the shadow of the fire several figures, or the rests of them: the sorry remnants of those *caxlan* come to wreak havoc on New Madagascar.

The efforts to complete the fleet of piraguas redoubled after that disastrous raid by Spanish mercenaries, and in the following weeks the shipyard became a furious hive of activity. Even in the black of night work proceeded by the flicker of torch-light.

❋

The moon went from dark to full before I spoke anew with Eaves, before we again circled around our shared longing.

This time it was I who raised the subject, late one night when the smoke of many fires was heavy on the air.

"It almost smells like London, doesn't it, where the air is so thick a decent family has to change their linens twice a day." I lingered next to Eaves as he tended the great bubbling pot of yucca and crawfish mixed with bitter greens that was the supper for the camp.

"It doesn't smell quite like London. Here we've got the musk of the swamp that drowns out any other scent, and in London there's the sharp smoke of coal that drifts on the air. You been thinking on London much lately, Surgeon?" Eaves asked.

"Not so much London in particular, seaman, but— thinking on the wide world, I suppose." Looking back, I think I said it playfully, almost coquettishly.

Eaves gave the bubbling pot a vigorous stir so the crawfish floated bright pink at the top. He took my arm and pulled me along with him.

"Walk with me a while, Surgeon; the pot will tend itself."

It was then that our conspiracy began in earnest—to my enduring regret, for look where I find myself: pleading for release or judgment from a dour tribunal, having lost my health and sanity in the bowels of this monstrous prison— this grasping beast that feeds on the lives of men, consuming each of their passing moments until it grows heavy and grey and slick, heaving and steaming over the delicacies of suffering and boredom.

As we walked Eaves put his arm through mine, and through the ragged sleeves of his shirt I could feel the scars that marked his passage through the world. Eaves told me then that he had been thinking how he was never pledged to live out the length of his days within the precincts of New Madagascar, only to safeguard the knowledge of its location and defenses. What was it if a man felt some attraction to the world, to the multitudes that live and swarm beneath the same sun on all the far-flung parts of the globe? What was it if a man looked at his own nature and found himself a wanderer, a citizen of the empire of dreams, or if he was beset by a curiosity that did not allow him to confine his energies within the bounds of one community?

"For some, their restless nature does not permit them to stay too long at the same place. And you, Surgeon—have you that desire that circles furiously in your gut like sharks around a bucket of chum?"

"I would describe it differently, but I think it is fair to say that at times I have an itch to see what is happening in the wider world, a feeling that has begun to burn and does not lose its heat."

Eaves proceeded to tell me of his conspiracy to slip away from New Madagascar along with two other co-conspirators, whom he would not name. The three of them lacked only one more set of shoulders to balance the boat and handle the paddle. Eaves spun for me a wishful tale of the ease of the escape: how the four conspirators could seize one of the piraguas to push through the surf before the first light of dawn, then make their way up the coast as the tides permitted, secure in the abundant provisions of the sea, pulling in to sleep at sheltered coves along the way before finally reaching a town at the edge of the civilized world, perhaps two weeks' hard paddling away. Once they had arrived at a far-off outpost they would spin an account of shipwreck or a jungle expedition gone awry to allow the establishment of new identities.

Having outlined his plan he asked me once again if I was feeling the pull of the world. I said yes but I said it with a sinking heart.

The plan that was struck required the members of the conspiracy to get down to the oceanside on the first transport so that we could slip away in the velvet hours of the night before the regular routines of security were established. As the preparations to transport the fleet of piraguas down to the shore neared their finish I fretted over how I would ensure my place on that first sortie. Being weak of back and no seaman, I had little to offer in the maneuvering of those lumbering ships through the winding and rocky rivulets that led down to the sea, and there was hardly any other reason for me to accompany the expedition.

That season there was a fever passing through the children of New Madagascar. It had taken away a few of them, to the lament of their parents and a great hue and cry among all the neighbors. The healers of the different traditions at New Madagascar drew on all manner of remedy and ritual, but still an anxious wail was heard every several days when another child was made still. I felt myself of slight use, as my cutting skills left me little to offer to those shivering out their last breaths.

I was conversing with Horacio under the glimmer of stars, as we were wont, when he told me of a similar illness that had passed through his village when he was a child. The cure was found in a powder made from grinding the spines of a luminescent fish that swims near the coral reef. I sat up stock-still when he said it and still feel the sting of regret that my first thought was of having found a premise of urgency to take me down to the oceanside, where I could harvest that medicine to fight the fever raging among the children of New Madagascar.

❋

The portage was brutal but accomplished without any complaint. It was a week of that rough party carefully floating those vessels down the river, steered by long ropes at the shore so they would not jump away. The piraguas were picked up and carried on determined shoulders through the thorny brush when the sides of the creek got too narrow. There were great woven sacks of supplies that were also hefted along; I was little help, being hard put with the hauling of my own kit. Once the operation was complete and the last piragua dragged down to the beach, Jalil and his gang got a wildness on them at being close to the sea, jumping around loose-limbed and rangy, whooping at the success of their enterprise as they tumbled in the dunes and the foamy splash.

Eaves came to shake me quietly as I lay sleepless and aggrieved at the thought of departing before having secured the remedy for the fever that haunted the families of New Madagascar. In the tumult of that first night neither Shelly nor Jalil had thought to post a guard, so as I made my way to follow Eaves there was only the light crackle of embers from the dying fire and the crash of the surf in the distance.

I made a last glance at the sleeping figures of Jeremiah and Jalil, curled up against each other like kittens taking a nap. The air was crisp, and the only light was the sliver of the moon. The wheel was set in motion. There was no option but to follow the round of its roll.

Eaves led me past a bank of dunes and it was there I first laid eyes on the other members of the conspiracy. One of them I recognized as a Welshman, a former pirate gone grey at the muzzle who had a sheepish expression. The other was a young son of New Madagascar with honey skin and hooded eyes that I thought carried a squint of contempt, but later when we talked he impressed me as quite kind and leaning to adventure out of simple curiosity.

As we pushed the small piragua through the surf in utter quiet I welcomed the splash and surge of the waves to wash away the signs of my weeping so my traitorous companions would not think me coward.

In the first days after that crepuscular stab into the pounding Atlantic surf the journey went smoothly. In no time our little party of miscreants found an alternating rhythm that propelled the piragua in a steady line northward, cruising along in the gentle waters about a hundred yards out past the surf. Navigation was a simple matter of keeping the rough coastline always to the left, a matter even I could track between the spasms that wracked my shoulders, unaccustomed as they were to hard labor. Towards the latter half of each day Eaves put out a line with some hooks to catch our evening meal, and when the sun came close to falling into the landward horizon we nosed the piragua in past the breakers to the beach, there to make a quick fire and cook some fish barely stopped wriggling off the hook, and then fall into a deep and unmoving sleep until the break of dawn, when Eaves would push us all up and onward.

At the onset of that doomed flight I could only look forward and work the paddle as hard as my muscles would permit in a vain attempt to hold off the nausea and tears that gripped me each and every time my thoughts rested on having left New Madagascar without bidding my friends farewell. I was surprised and forlorn that Jalil did not send out a party to apprehend us. Each morning while my eyes were still closed I hoped to awake again to a spear-point at my side as we had in those first days after the wreck of the Revenge. I yearned to find myself admonished for the turn of my back against the feverish children of New Madagascar and against my companions, around whom I had stretched the tendrils of affection.

It was the fifth day when disaster struck. The day began, rosy dawn creeping up above the edge of the Atlantic with its steady sweetness, the air crisp and silent but for the splash of the waves at low tide and the slight and distant cry of gulls scanning the surf for their breakfast. The sun was barely at its zenith when a sudden wave surged across the piragua and quick as a heartbeat knocked the ship over, flinging all of our supplies to sink like stones into the watery deep and along with them the Welshman, who scarcely murmured before he too was dragged down. The poor man had never learned to swim.

Eaves and I and the young Madagascan clung, stunned, to the hull of our overturned vessel. It was the Madagasacan who noted, with a rising panic, that there was a current pulling us quickly out into the wastes, measurable by the growing distance to the shoreline with its crown of waving palms teasing and beckoning in the receding distance.

Eaves and the Madagascan debated attempting to swim to shore, for we had lost our paddles in that sudden surge and there remained no way to direct the piragua without them. I stayed out of the conversation, knowing it was impossible I would make that long crossing and that my only option was to cling desperately to the overturned piragua. Eaves made his calculations and figured the same, but our young companion struck out towards the shore. Within the hour we saw his bobbing head disappear below the waves forever.

Eaves and I managed to right the boat, but without the paddles to direct our course, and having lost the bladders full of fresh water and even the line and hooks that Eaves had used to catch those darting fish, we were quickly reduced to delirium. It was in delirium that we were found adrift after endless days barely marked by the alternation of moon and sun passing across the vault of the sky.

As soon as Eaves saw the approach of the navy ship he shook himself to waking and shouted out with a sudden, lucid fury, "My days of chaining are long behind me. Good luck to you, Surgeon!" And he slipped overboard to swim off as best he could. I think it was a shark that took him with a quick jerk, because the water bloomed crimson around where he was pulled down.

That, finally, is where I was taken, to be transported through a long chain of custody whose final link leaves me here before you, begging your higher graces that you might see: although I found those pirates beautiful and brave, I did not take part in their conspiracy.

You may render what lessons you will from my little tale, but let me leave you with a caution. Should you make any attempt to extinguish the maroons of New Madagascar in their swampy refuge, be warned: they stand ready and their knives are drawn.

THE END

FURTHER READING

Books

Cordingly, David. *Under the Black Flag: The Romance and the Reality of Life among the Pirates.* New York: Random House, 2006.

Davidson, Basil. *The Black Man's Burden: Africa and the Curse of the Nation-State.* New York: Times Books, 1992.

Earle, Peter. *The Pirate Wars.* New York: Thomas Dunne Books, 2003.

Equiano, Olaudah. *The Interesting Narrative of the Life of Olaudah Equiano, or, Gustavus Vassa, the African.* New York: Modern Library, 2004.

Galindo, Alberto Flores. *In Search of an Inca: Identity and Utopia in the Andes.* Cambridge: Cambridge University Press, 2010.

Gonzalez-Crussi, F. *A Short History of Medicine.* New York: Modern Library, 2007.

Johnson, Captain Charles. *A General History of the Robberies and Murders of the Most Notorious Pirates.* New York: Lyons Press, 2002.

Linebaugh, Peter. *The Magna Carta Manifesto.* Berkeley, CA: University of California Press, 2008.

——— and Marcus Rediker. *The Many-Headed Hydra: Sailors, Slaves, Commoners, and the Hidden History of the Revolutionary Atlantic.* Boston: Beacon Press, 2000.

Little, Benerson. *The Sea Rover's Practice: Pirate Tactics and Techniques 1630–1730.* Lincoln, NE: Potomac Books, 2005.

Mintz, Sidney W. *Sweetness and Power: The Place of Sugar in Modern History.* New York: Penguin Books, 1986.

Price, Richard. *Maroon Societies: Rebel Slave Communities in the Americas.* New York: Anchor Books, 1973.

———. *To Slay the Hydra: Dutch Colonial Perspectives on the Saramaka Wars.* Ann Arbor, MI: Karoma Publishers, 1983.

Rediker, Marcus. *Between the Devil and the Deep Blue Sea: Merchant Seamen, Pirates, and the Anglo-American Maritime World 1700–1750.* Cambridge: Cambridge University Press, 1987.

———. *The Slave Ship: A Human History.* New York: Penguin Books, 2007.

———. *Villains of All Nations: Atlantic Pirates in the Golden Age.* Boston: Beacon Press, 2004.

Shapin, Steven. *The Scientific Revolution.* Chicago: University of Chicago Press, 1998.

Various. *The Pirate's Own Book: Authentic Narratives of the Most Celebrated Sea Robbers.* Mineola, NY: Dover Publications, 1993.

Williams, Eric. *From Columbus to Castro: The History of the Caribbean 1492–1969.* New York: Vintage Books, 1984.

Wilson, Peter Lamborn. *Pirate Utopias: Moorish Corsairs and European Renegades.* New York: Autonomedia, 1995.

Woodard, Colin. *The Republic of Pirates: Being the True and Surprising Story of the Caribbean Pirates and the Man Who Brought Them Down.* Boston: Mariner Books, 2007.

Wright, Ronald. *Stolen Continents: Conquest and Resistance in the Americas.* Boston: Mariner Books, 1993.

Articles

Anderson, Robert Nelson. "The Quilombo of Palmares: A New Overview of a Mároon State in Seventeenth Century Brazil." *Journal of Latin American Studies* 28:3, Brazil: History and Society (October 1996), 545–66.

Aptheker, Herbert. "Maroons Within the Present Limits of the United States." *The Journal of Negro History* 24:2 (April 1939) 167–84.

Beattie, J.M. "The Criminality of Women in Eighteenth-Century England." *Journal of Social History* 8:4 (Summer 1975), 80–116.

Bilby, Kenneth. "Swearing by the Past, Swearing to the Future: Sacred Oaths, Alliances, and Treaties among the Guainese and Jamaican Maroons." *Ethnohistory* 44:4 (Autumn 1997), 655–89.

Brown, Chandos Michael. "A Natural History of the Gloucester Sea Serpent: Knowledge, Power, and the Culture of Science in Antebellum America." *American Quarterly* 42:3 (September 1990), 402–36.

Carroll, Patrick J. "Mandinga: The Evolution of a Mexican Runaway Slave Community 1735–1827." *Comparative Studies in Society and History* 19:4 (October 1977), 488–505.

Fussell, G.E. "English Countryside and Population in the Eighteenth Century." *Economic Geography* 12:3 (July 1936), 294–310.

———. "The Size of English Cattle in the Eighteenth Century." *Agricultural History* 3:4 (October 1929), 160–81.

Gay, Edwin F. "The Inclosure Movement in England." *Publications of the American Economic Association*, Third Series 6:2, *Papers and Proceedings of the Seventeenth Annual Meeting*, Part II (May 1905), 146–59.

Grafton, R. Quentin. "Governance of the Commons: A Role for the State?" *Land Economics* 76:4 (November 2000), 504–17.

Halliday, M.A.K. "Anti-Languages." *American Anthropologist*, New Series 78:3 (September 1976), 570–84.

Humphries, Jane. "Enclosures, Common Rights, and Women: The Proletarianization of Families in the Late Eighteenth and Early Nineteenth Centuries." *The Journal of Economic History* 50:1 (March 1990), 17–42.

Kopytoff, Barbara Klaymon. "The Early Political Development of Jamaican Maroon Societies." *The William and Mary Quarterly*, Third Series 35:2 (April 1978), 287–307.

Lemisch, Jesse. "Jack Tar in the Streets: Merchant Seamen in the Politics of Revolutionary America." *The William and Mary Quarterly*, Third Series 25:3 (July 1968), 371–407.

Masson, Marilyn A. "Postclassic Maya Communities at Progresso Lagoon and Laguna Seca, Northern Belize." *Journal of Field Archaeology* 26:3 (Autumn 1999), 285–306.

McDonald, Dedra S. "Intimacy and Empire: Indian-African Interactions in Spanish Colonial New Mexico 1500-1800." *American Indian Quarterly* 22:1-2 (Winter-Spring 1998), 134–56.

Newman, L.F. "Some Notes on Food and Dietetics in the Sixteenth and Seventeenth Centuries." *The Journal of the Royal Anthropological Institute of Great Britain and Ireland* 76:1 (1946), 39–49.

Newman, Simon P. "Reading the Bodies of Early American Seafarers." *The William and Mary Quarterly*, Third Series 55:1 (January 1998), pp 59–82.

Plumb, J.H. "The New World of Children in Eighteenth Century England." *Past and Present* 67 (May 1975), 64–95.

Prentice, E. Parmalee. "Food in England." *Agricultural History* 24:2 (April 1950), 65–70.

Rediker, Marcus. "'Under the Banner of King Death': The Social World of Anglo-American Pirates." *The William and Mary Quarterly*, Third Series 38:2 (April 1981), 203–27.

Rude, George. "The London 'Mob' of the Eighteenth Century." *The Historical Journal*, 2:1 (1950), 1–18.

Sabine, Ernest L. "Butchering in Mediaeval London." *Speculum* 8:3 (July 1933), 335–53.

Super, John C. "Food and History." *Journal of Social History* 36:1 (Autumn 2002), 165–78.

Wordie, J.R. "The Chronology of English Enclosure 1500–1914." *The Economic History Review*, New Series 35:4 (November 1983), 483–505.

ABOUT THE AUTHOR

Tauno Biltsted has been a cab driver, squatter on the Lower East Side of Manhattan, mediator and facilitator, and roustabout construction worker. His fiction has been published in *Rosebud Magazine* and the Akashic Books *Mondays are Murder* series, and his nonfiction has been published in *World War 3 Illustrated, Wobblies!: A Graphic History of the IWW*, and *Perspectives on Anarchist Theory*. He holds a master's degree in International Relations.